A crackle of lightning flickered across the thickening darkness, illuminating the small but steep hill that marked the deepest part of the forest. Nyberg looked up and saw a tall figure silhouetted against the trees at the crest of the hill, someone in a long coat or robe, the dark fabric rippling in the wind. The figure raised long arms to the raging sky—

—and the stutter of lightning was gone, plunging the strange, dramatic scene back into darkness.

"What the—" Nyberg began, and more water splashed across the glass—except it wasn't water, because water didn't stick in great, dark clumps, water didn't ooze, and break apart, revealing dozens of shining needle teeth. Nyberg blinked, not sure what he was seeing as someone started to scream at the other end of the car, a long, rising wail, as more of the dark, slug-like creatures, each the size of a man's fist, smashed against the window. The sound of hail on the roof went from a patter to a storm, the thunder of it drowning out the screamer, the screams of many now.

Hot panic shot through Nyberg's body, sending him to his feet. He made it to the aisle before the glass behind him shattered, before glass all through the train was shattering, the high, jagged sound of it melding with the screams of terror, all of it nearly lost beneath the ongoing thunder of attack. As the lights went out, something cold and wet and very much alive landed on the back of his neck and began to feed.

POCKET FICTION BY S.D. PERRY

RESIDENT EVIL
ZERO HOUR

S.D. PERRY

POCKET STAR BOOKS
New York   London   Toronto   Sydney

An *Original* Publication of POCKET BOOKS

 A Pocket Star Book published by
POCKET BOOKS, a division of Simon & Schuster, Inc.
1230 Avenue of the Americas, New York, NY 10020

ISBN 13: 978-0-671-78511-6
ISBN 10:   0-671-78511-7

First Pocket Books printing November 2004

10 9 8 7 6

Cover art by Mark Gerber

Manufactured in the United States of America

For information regarding special discounts for bulk purchases, please contact Simon & Schuster Special Sales at 1-800-456-6798 or business@simonandschuster.com.

AUTHOR'S NOTE

Faithful readers of this series have probably already read this note, but please allow me to repeat myself: You may notice time and/or character discrepencies between the books and the games (or the books and the books, for that matter). With the games, comics, and novelizations being written, revised, and produced at different times and by different people, complete consistency is impossible. I can only apologize on behalf of us all, and hope that in spite of chronological errors, you will continue to enjoy the mix of corporate zombies and hapless heroes that makes Resident Evil so much fun—to write, and, if I'm lucky, to read.

For Mÿk and Cy, my boys.

Hunger for power is evil's true root.

—*Judith Moriae*

PROLOGUE

The train swayed and rocked as it traveled through the Raccoon woods, the thunder of its wheels echoed by a thundering twilight sky.

Bill Nyberg rifled through the Hardy file, his briefcase on the floor at his feet. It had been a long day, and the gentle rocking of the train soothed him. It was late, after eight, but the Ecliptic Express was mostly full, as it often was for the dinner hour. It was a company train, and since the renovation—Umbrella had gone to great expense to make it classically retro, everything from velvet seats to chandeliers in the dining car—a lot of employees brought family or friends along to experience the atmosphere. There were usually a number of out-of-towners on board as well,

S. D. PERRY

having caught the connection out of Latham, but Nyberg would have bet that nine out of ten of them worked for Umbrella, too. Without the pharmaceutical giant's support, Raccoon City wouldn't even be a wide spot in the road.

One of the car attendants walked past, nodding at Nyberg when he saw the Umbrella pin on his lapel. The small pin marked him as a regular commuter. Nyberg nodded back. A flicker of lightning outside was quickly followed by another rumble of thunder; it seemed there was a summer storm brewing. Even in the cool comfort of the train, the air seemed charged, thick with the tension of impending rain.

And my coat is . . . in the trunk? Wonderful. His car was at the far end of the station lot, too. He'd be drenched before he got halfway across.

Sighing, he returned his attention to the file, settling back into his seat. He'd already reviewed the material a number of times, but he wanted to be on top of every detail. A ten-year-old girl named Teresa Hardy had been involved in a clinical trial for a new pediatric heart medication, Valifin. As it turned out, the drug did exactly what it was supposed to do—but it also caused renal failure, and in Teresa Hardy's case, the damage had been severe. She'd survive, but would likely spend the rest of her life on dialysis, and the family's lawyer was seeking hefty damages. The case had to be settled quickly, the Hardy family kept quiet before they could drag their ailing, cherub-cheeked moppet in front of a media-packed courtroom . . . which was where Nyberg and his team came in. The trick was to offer just enough to make the family happy, but not so much as to encourage their lawyer—one of those strip-mall, "we don't get paid unless you get paid" outfits—to get greedy. Nyberg had a knack for handling ambulance chasers; he'd have it settled before little Teresa got back from her first treatment. It was what Umbrella paid him for.

Rain splattered loudly against the window, as though someone had thrown a bucket of water against the pane. Startled, Nyberg turned to look out, just as several dull thumps sounded on the train's roof. Terrific. Had to be a hailstorm or something . . .

A crackle of lightning flickered across the thickening darkness, illuminating the small but steep hill that marked the deepest part of the forest. Nyberg looked up, and saw a tall figure silhouetted against the trees at the crest of the hill, someone in a long coat or robe, the dark fabric rippling in the wind. The figure raised long arms to the raging sky—

—and the stutter of lightning was gone, plunging the strange, dramatic scene back into darkness.

"What the—" Nyberg began, and more water splashed across the glass—except it wasn't water, because water didn't stick in great, dark clumps;

3

water didn't ooze and break apart, revealing dozens of shining needle teeth. Nyberg blinked, not sure what he was seeing as someone started to scream at the other end of the car, a long, rising wail, as more of the dark, sluglike creatures, each the size of a man's fist, smashed against the window. The sound of hail on the roof went from a patter to a storm, the thunder of it drowning out the screamer, the screams of many now.

Not hail, that's not hail!

Hot panic shot through Nyberg's body, sending him to his feet. He made it to the aisle before the glass behind him shattered, before glass all through the train was shattering, the high, jagged sound of it melding with the screams of terror, all of it nearly lost beneath the ongoing thunder of attack. As the lights went out, something cold and wet and very much alive landed on the back of his neck and began to feed.

ONE

The helicopter spun through the darkness over Raccoon forest.

Rebecca Chambers sat up straight, willing herself to look as calm as the men around her. The mood was solemn, as dark and clouded as the skies whipping past, all jokes and jabs left behind at the briefing. This wasn't a training exercise. Three more people, hikers, had gone missing—in a forest as large as the one surrounding Raccoon, not that unusual—but with the rash of savage murders that had terrorized the small city over the past several weeks, "missing" had taken on new meaning. Only a few days earlier there'd been a ninth victim found, this one as ripped up and savaged as if it had been run through a meat grinder. People were being killed, savagely attacked by someone or some thing around the outskirts of the city, and the Raccoon police weren't getting anywhere. The city's chapter of S.T.A.R.S. had finally been called in to investigate.

Rebecca raised her chin slightly, a pulse of pride edging through her nervousness. Although her degree was in biochemistry, she'd been tapped as Bravo team's field medic, joining the team less than a month earlier.

My first mission. Which means I'd better not cock it up. She took a deep breath, letting it out slowly, working to keep her expression casual.

Edward shot her an encouraging smile, and Sully leaned across the crowded cabin to reassuringly pat her leg. So much for looking cool. As smart as she was, as ready as she was to begin her career, she couldn't help her age, or the fact that she looked even younger. At eighteen, she was the youngest person to be accepted into the S.T.A.R.S. since its creation in 1967 . . . and as the only female on Raccoon's B team, everyone treated her like their kid sister.

She sighed, smiling back at Edward, nodding at Sully. It wasn't so bad, having a handful of hardass big brothers watching out for her—as long as they understood she could take care of herself when the need arose.

I think, she silently amended. It was her first assignment, after all, and though she was in good shape physically, her combat experience had been limited to video simulations and weekend missions. The Special Tactics and Rescue Service wanted her in their labs, eventually, but field time was mandatory and she needed the experience. Anyway, they'd be sweeping the woods as a team. If they did run across the people or animals that had been attacking Raccoon's citizens, she'd have backup.

There was a flicker of lightning to the north, close, the subsequent thunder lost to the drone of the 'copter. Rebecca leaned forward slightly, scanning the dark. It had been clear all day, the clouds rolling in just before sunset; they were definitely going to go home wet. At least it would be a warm rain; she supposed it could be a lot—

Boom!

She'd been so focused on the coming storm that for a crazed split second, she thought it was thunder, even as the helicopter tipped wildly and dropped, a terrible rising, clattering whine filling the cabin, the floor vibrating beneath her boots. A hot smell of burned metal and ozone singed her nose.

Lightning?

"What happened?" someone shouted. Enrico, riding shotgun.

"Engine failure!" The pilot, Kevin Dooley, shouted back. "Emergency landing!"

Rebecca grabbed a strut and held on, looked to the others so she wouldn't have to watch the trees rushing up at them. She saw the grim, determined set to Sully's jaw, Edward's clenched teeth, the look of anxiety shot between Richard and Forest as they grabbed for struts or handholds on the shuddering wall. In the front, Enrico was shouting something else, something she couldn't make out over the scream of the dying engine. Rebecca closed her eyes for a beat, thought of her parents—and then the ride was too wild for her to think, the crack and crash of tree branches battering the helicopter too loud and jarring for her to do anything but hope. The 'copter spun out of control, whipping around in a tilting, sickening, lurching circle.

It was over a second later, the silence so sudden and complete that she thought she'd gone deaf, all movement stopped. Then she heard the tick of metal, the strangled last gasp of the engine, and her own thundering heart, and realized that they were down. Kevin had done it, and without a single bounce.

"Everyone okay?" Enrico Marini, their captain, was craned around in his seat.

Rebecca added her own shaky nod to the chorus of affirmations.

"Nice flying, Kev," Forest said, and there was another chorus. Rebecca couldn't have agreed more.

"Is the radio down?" Enrico asked the pilot, who was tapping at controls and flipping switches.

"Looks like everything electrical is fried," Kevin said. "It must have been lightning. We weren't struck directly, but it was close enough. Beacon, too."

"Can it be repaired?"

Enrico addressed it as an open question, looking at Richard, their communications officer. Richard in turn looked at Edward, who shrugged. Edward was the Bravo team's mechanic.

"I'll take a look," Edward said, "but if Kev says the transmitter's toast, it's probably toast."

The captain nodded slowly, absently brushing at his mustache with one hand as he considered their options. After a few seconds, he sighed. "I called in when we were hit, but I don't know if it went through," he said. "They'll have our last coordinates, though. If we don't report in pretty soon, they'll come looking."

"They" was the S.T.A.R.S. Alpha team. Rebecca nodded along with the others, not sure if she should be disappointed or not. Her first mission, over before it started.

Enrico wiped at his mustache again, smoothing it down at the corners of his mouth with the thumb and forefinger of one hand. "Everybody out. Let's see where we are."

They filed out of the cabin, the reality of the situation hitting Rebecca as they gathered together in the dark. They were incredibly lucky to be alive.

Struck by lightning. On our way to search for mad killers, no less, she thought, amazed at the very idea. Even if the mission was over, this was hands down the most exciting thing that had ever happened to her.

The air was warm and heavy with impending rain, the shadows deep. Small animals rustled through the underbrush. A pair of flashlights clicked on, the beams cutting through the dark as Enrico and Edward moved around the helicopter, examining the damage. Rebecca fished her own flashlight out of her bag, relieved that she hadn't forgotten to pack it.

"How you holding up?"

Rebecca turned, saw Ken "Sully" Sullivan grinning down at her. He had his weapon out, the nine-millimeter's muzzle pointed to the overcast sky, a grim reminder of why they were there in the first place.

"You guys really know how to make an entrance, don't you?" she said, smiling back at him.

The tall man laughed, his teeth very white against the darkness of his skin. "Actually, we always do this for the new recruits. It's a waste of helicopters, but we have our reputation to maintain."

She was about to ask how the police chief felt about the expense—she was new to the area, but she'd heard that Chief Irons was notoriously stingy—when Enrico joined them, pulling his own weapon and raising his voice so everyone could hear.

"All right, people. Let's fan out, investigate the surrounding area. Kev, stay with the 'copter. The rest of you, keep close, I just want this area secured. Alpha could be here in as little as an hour."

He didn't complete the thought, that it could be a hell of a lot longer, but he didn't need to. For the moment, at least, they were on their own.

Rebecca slid the nine-millimeter out of its holster, carefully checking the magazine and chamber as she'd been taught, raising the muzzle to avoid inadvertently aiming at anyone. The others were moving out to either side, checking weapons and turning on flashlights. She took a deep breath and started to walk straight ahead, swinging the flashlight's beam around in front of her. Enrico was only a few meters away, moving parallel to her position. A low mist had cropped up, wafting through the underbrush like a ghostly tide. There was a parting in the trees about a dozen meters ahead, a path big enough to be a narrow road, though it was hard to tell for the mist. It was quiet except for a rumble of thunder, the sound closer than she would have expected; the storm was almost upon them. She swept the beam across trees and darkness and trees again, then a glint of what looked like—

"Captain, look!"

Enrico stepped to her side, and within seconds, five more beams of light had jerked toward the gleam of metal she'd seen, illuminating what was, in fact, a narrow dirt road—and an overturned jeep. Rebecca could see MP etched on the side as the team moved closer. Military police. She saw a pile of clothes spilling out from beneath the shattered windshield and frowned, stepping in for a better look—and then she was holstering her weapon and fumbling for her medkit, hurrying over to kneel next to the crashed jeep, knowing even before she sat back on her heels that there was nothing she could do. There was too much blood.

Two men. One had been thrown clear, was crumpled a few meters away. The other, the fair-haired man in front of her, was still half under the jeep. Both wore military fatigues. Their faces and upper bodies had been badly mutilated. There were massive tears through skin and muscle, deep gashes across their throats. No way the crash had done all of it.

Rebecca reflexively reached down and felt for a pulse, noting the chill of the flesh. She stood and moved to the other body, again checking for any sign of life, but he was as cold as the first.

"You think they're from Ragithon?" someone asked. Richard. Rebecca saw a briefcase near the pale, outstretched hand of the second corpse and crouch-walked to it, half listening to Enrico's answer as she flipped the case's lid.

"It's the closest base, but look at the insignia. They're jarheads. Could be from Donnell," Enrico said.

A clipboard was on top of a handful of files, an official looking document attached to it. There was a small headshot in the upper left corner, of a handsome, dark-eyed young man in civvies—neither of the corpses looked like him. Rebecca lifted it out, reading silently—and then her mouth went dry.

"Captain!" she managed, standing.

Enrico looked up from where he was crouched, next to the jeep. "Hmm? What happened?"

She read the pertinent parts aloud. " 'Court order for transportation . . . prisoner William Coen, ex-lieutenant, twenty-six years old. Court-martialed and sentenced to death, July 22nd. Prisoner is to be transferred to the Ragithon base for execution.' " The lieutenant had been convicted of first-degree murder.

Edward pulled the clipboard from her hands, saying what was already formulating in Rebecca's mind, his voice heavy with anger. "Those poor soldiers. They were just doing their jobs, and that scum murdered them and escaped."

Enrico took the clipboard away from him, scanning it quickly. "All right, everyone. Change of plan. We may have an escaped killer on our hands. Let's separate and survey the immediate area, see if we can't locate Lieutenant Billy. Keep your guard up, and report back in fifteen, regardless."

There were nods all around. Rebecca took a deep breath as the others started to move out, checking her watch, determined to be as professional as anyone else on the team. Fifteen minutes alone, no big deal. What could happen in fifteen minutes? Alone. In the dark, dark woods.

"Got your radio?"

Rebecca jumped and turned at the sound of Edward's voice, the big man standing directly behind her. The mechanic patted her on the shoulder, smiling.

"Easy, kiddo."

Rebecca smiled back at him, though she despised being called "kiddo." Edward was only twenty-six, for God's sake. She tapped the unit on her belt.

"Check."

Edward nodded, stepping away. His message was clear, and reassuring. She wasn't really alone, not as long as she had her radio. She looked around, saw that the several of the others were already out of sight. Kevin, still in the pilot's seat, was going through the briefcase that she'd found. He saw her and snapped her a salute. Rebecca gave him a thumbs-up and squared her shoulders, drawing her weapon once more and heading out into the night. Overhead, thunder rumbled.

Albert Wesker sat in the treatment plant's Con B1, the room dark except for the flicker from a bank of observation monitors, six of them, each changing view on five-second rotations. There were shots from every level of the training facility, the upper and lower floors of the factory and water treatment plant, and the tunnel that connected the two. He gazed at the soundless black-and-white screens without really looking at them; most of his attention was focused on the incoming transmissions from the cleanup crew. The three-man team—well, two and a pilot— was en route by 'copter, and mostly silent; they were professionals, after all, not given to macho banter or juvenile jokes, which meant Wesker was hearing a lot of static. That was all right; the white noise went well with the blank and staring faces he saw on the monitors, the ravaged bodies slumped in corners, the men who'd been infected shambling aimlessly through empty corridors. Like the Arklay mansion and labs only a few miles away, White Umbrella's private training grounds and connected facilities had been hit by the virus.

"ETA thirty minutes, over," the pilot said, his voice crackling through the dimly lit room.

Wesker leaned in. "Copy that."

Silence again. There was no need to talk about what would happen when they reached the train . . . and though the channel was scrambled, it was best not to say more than was necessary, anyway. Umbrella had been built on a foundation of secrecy, a characteristic of the pharmaceutical giant that was still honored by everyone in the upper echelons of management. Even in the company's legitimate dealings, the less said the better.

It's all coming down, Wesker thought idly, watching the screens. Spencer's mansion and the surrounding labs had gone down in the middle of May. White Umbrella's take on it had been "accidental," the lab locked down until the infected researchers and staff became "ineffective." Mistakes happened, after all. But the training facility nightmare that was still playing out in front of him had followed not a month later . . . and only a few hours ago, the engineer of Umbrella's private train, the Ecliptic Express, had pushed the biohazard panic button.

So, the lockdown didn't work, the virus leaked and spread. It's that simple . . . isn't it?

There were a handful of infected grunts in the training facility's dining room, one of them walking in looping circles around the once-handsome table. He was leaking some viscous fluid out of a nasty head wound as he staggered along, oblivious to his whereabouts, to pain, to everything. Wesker tapped at the control panel beneath the monitor, keeping the surveillance from moving to the next picture. He sat back in his chair, watching the doomed walker as he circled the table yet again.

"Sabotage, maybe," he said softly. He couldn't be sure. It was set up to look natural—a spill at the Arklay lab, an incomplete lockdown. A few weeks later, a couple of missing hikers, likely caused by an escaped test subject or two, and a few weeks more, infection at a second White Umbrella facility. It was highly improbable that one of the virus carriers would just happen to blunder their way to one of Raccoon's other labs, but it was possible . . . except now there was the train to consider. And it didn't feel like an accident. It felt . . . planned.

Hell, I might have done it myself, if I'd thought of it. He'd been looking for a way out for some time now, tired of working for people who were obviously his inferiors . . . and well aware that too much time on White Umbrella's payroll wasn't good for the health. Now they wanted him to lead the S.T.A.R.S. into the Arklay mansion and labs, to find out just how well Umbrella's war pets fared against armed soldiers. Did they give a shit if he died in the process? Not so long as he recorded the data first, he was sure.

Researchers, doctors, techs—anyone who worked

for White Umbrella for more than a decade or two
had a habit of winding up missing or dead, eventually. George Trevor and his family, Dr. Marcus,
Dees, Dr. Darius, Alexander Ashford . . . and those
were just some of the bigger names. God only knew
how many of the little people had ended up in shallow graves somewhere . . . or turned up as test subjects A, B, and C.

The corner of Wesker's mouth twitched. Come to
think of it, *he* had a fairly good idea of how many.
He'd been working for White Umbrella since the late
seventies, most of that in the Raccoon area, and had
watched the docs run through quite a few test subjects, many he had helped procure himself. It was well
past his time to get out . . . and if he could get the data
the big boys wanted, he might just be able to throw
himself a little bidding war, a going-away present to
fund his retirement. White Umbrella wasn't the only
group interested in bioweapons research.

But first a cleanup for the train. *And this place,*
he thought, watching as the soldier with the head
wound tripped over a chair leg and went down hard.
The training facility was connected to the "private"
water treatment plant by an underground tunnel; it
would all have to be cleared.

A few seconds passed, and the soldier onscreen
staggered to his feet again, continuing on his mindless quest to nowhere . . . and now there appeared to

be a dinner fork sticking out of his upper right shoulder, a little souvenir from his fall. The soldier didn't notice, of course. A charming little disease. It had been the same kind of scene at the Arklay labs, Wesker was sure; the last few desperate phone calls from the quarantined lab had painted a vivid picture of just how effective the T-virus really was. That would have to be cleaned up, too . . . but not until after he got the S.T.A.R.S. out there for a little training exercise.

It would be an interesting match. The S.T.A.R.S. were good—he'd handpicked half of them himself—but they'd never seen anything like the T-virus. The dying soldier on the screen was a prime example—hot with the recombinant virus, he went on with his endless tour of the dining room, slow and mostly brainless. He also felt no pain—and he would attack anyone or anything that happened across his path with no hesitation, the virus continually seeking new hosts to infect. Although the original spill was allegedly airborne, after this long, the virus would only be spread by bodily fluids. By blood, or, say, a bite . . . And the soldier was just a man, after all; the T-virus worked on all manners of living tissue, and there were a number of other . . . animals . . . to see in action, from laboratory triumphs to local wildlife.

Enrico should have the Bravos out by now, searching for the latest missing hikers, but it was doubtful they'd find anything where he was planning to look. Sometime soon, Wesker would see about organizing an Alpha-Bravo camp-out at the "deserted" Spencer mansion. Then he'd wipe out the evidence and be on his merry, wealthy way, to hell with White Umbrella, to hell with his life as a double-agent, playing with the petty lives of men and women he didn't give a shit about.

The dying man on the screen fell down once again, dragged himself to his feet, and soldiered on.

"Go for the gold, baby," Wesker said, and chuckled, the sound echoing out through the empty dark.

Something moved in the bushes. Something bigger than a squirrel.

Rebecca spun toward the sound, aiming the flashlight and nine-millimeter at the shrub. The light caught the last of the movement, the leaves still shaking, the beam from her flashlight trembling along with them. She took a step closer, swallowing dryly, counting backward from ten. Whatever it was, it was gone now.

A raccoon, is all. Or maybe somebody's dog got loose.

She looked at her watch, sure that it must be time to head back, and saw that she'd been on her own for just over five minutes. She hadn't seen or heard anyone else since she'd walked away from the helicopter; it was as though everyone else had fallen off the face of the earth.

Or I have, she thought darkly, lowering the handgun slightly, turning to check her position. She'd been heading roughly southwest from the landing point; she'd continue on a few more minutes, then—

Rebecca blinked, surprised to see a metal wall beneath the flashlight's beam, not ten meters away. She played the light across the surface, saw windows, a door—

"A train," she breathed, frowning slightly. It seemed like she remembered something about a track up here . . . Umbrella, the pharmaceutical corporation, had a private line that ran from Latham to Raccoon City, didn't they? She wasn't too certain on the history—she wasn't a local—but she was pretty sure the company had been founded in Raccoon. Umbrella's headquarters had moved off to Europe some time ago, but they still owned practically the entire town.

So what's it doing sitting up here, dead in the woods at this time of night? She ran the light up and down the train, saw that there were five tall cars, each two stories high. ECLIPTIC EXPRESS was written just below the roof of the car in front of her. There were a few lights on, but they were faint, barely casting through the windows . . . several of which were broken. She thought she saw a person's silhouette near one of the unbroken ones, but it wasn't moving. Someone asleep, maybe.

Or hurt, or dead. Maybe this thing is stopped because Billy Coen found his way onto the track.

God, that was a thought. He could be inside now, with hostages. She should definitely call for backup. She started to reach for her radio, then paused.

Or maybe the train broke down two weeks ago and it's been here ever since, and all you'll find inside is a colony of woodchucks. Wouldn't the team have a laugh over that? They'd be nice about it, but she'd have to endure weeks, maybe months of gentle ribbing, calling for backup over a deserted train.

She checked her watch again, saw that two minutes had passed since the last check . . . and felt a drop of cool liquid splash on her nose. Then another on her arm. Then the soft, musical patter of a hundred drops against leaves and dirt, then thousands as the sky opened up, the storm finally beginning.

The rain decided it for her; a quick look inside before she headed back, just to make sure everything was the way it was supposed to be. If Billy wasn't around, she'd at least be able to report back that the train appeared to be clear. And if he was . . .

"You'll have to deal with me," she murmured, the sound lost to the growing storm as she approached the silent train.

†wo

Billy sat on the floor between two rows of seats, working at the handcuffs with a paper clip he'd found on the floor. One of the cuffs was off, the right one, bashed open when the jeep had gone over, but unless he wanted to be wearing a jangly and rather incriminating bracelet, he had to get the other one off.

Get it off and get the hell out of here, he thought, pushing at the lock with the thin piece of metal. He didn't look up, didn't need to remind himself of his whereabouts; he didn't have to. The air was heavy with the scent of blood, it was splattered all over the place, and although the train car he'd found was empty of bodies, he had no doubt that the other cars were full of them.

The dogs, has to be those dogs . . . though who let them on?

The same guy they'd seen in the woods, had to be. The guy who'd stepped in front of the jeep, sending it crashing out of control. Billy had been thrown clear and except for a few bruises, was pretty much unscathed. His MP escort, Dickson and Elder, had both been trapped beneath the overturned vehicle. They'd been alive, though. The human roadstop, whoever he was, was nowhere to be seen.

It had been a tough minute or two, standing there in the gathering dark, the hot, oily smell of gas in his face, his body aching, trying to decide—run for it, or radio for help? He didn't want to die, didn't *deserve* to die, unless being trusting and stupid was an offense worthy of death. But he couldn't leave them, either, two men pinned under a ton of twisted metal, injured and barely conscious. Their choice, to take some unpaved backwoods trail to the base, meant it could be a long time before anyone happened upon them. Yeah, they were delivering him to his execution, but they were following orders; it wasn't personal, and they didn't deserve to die any more than he did.

He'd decided to split the difference, radio for help, then run like hell . . . but then the dogs had come. Big, wet, freaky looking things, three of them, and then he was running for his life, because there was something very, very wrong about them; he knew it even before they'd attacked Dickson, ripping his throat out as they pulled him from beneath the jeep.

Billy thought he heard a *click* and tried the handcuff, hissing air through his teeth when the metal latch refused to budge. Goddamn thing. The paper clip was a lucky find, though there was shit everywhere—papers, bags, coats, personal belongings—and blood on just about all of it. Maybe he'd find something more useful, if he looked harder . . . though that would mean staying on the train, and that didn't sound like much fun at all. For all he knew, this was where those dogs lived, holed up here with that crazy asshole who liked to step in front of moving cars. He'd only come aboard to avoid the dogs, to regroup, try and figure out his next move.

And it turns out to be the Slaughterhouse Special, he thought, shaking his head. *Talk about out of the frying pan, into the fire.* Whatever the hell was going on out in these woods, he didn't want to be a part of it. He'd get the cuff off, find himself some kind of weapon, maybe grab a wallet or two out of all the blood-splattered luggage—he had no doubt that the owners were long past caring—and hightail it back to civilization. Then Canada, or Mexico, maybe. He'd never stolen before, never considered leaving the country, but he had to think like a criminal now, if he wanted to survive.

He heard thunder, then gentle taps of rain against some of the unbroken windows. The taps became a tattoo, the blood-scented air thinning with a gust of wind through a shattered pane. Dandy. Apparently, he'd be hiking out in a rainstorm.

"Whatever," he mumbled, and threw the useless paper clip against the seat in front of him. The situation was seriously FUBAR, he doubted it could get much worse—

Billy froze, held his breath. The outside door to the train was opening. He could hear the metal sliding, the rain getting louder, then quieter again. Someone had come aboard.

Shit! What if it was the maniac with the dogs?

Or what if someone found the jeep?

He felt a sick, heavy knot in his stomach. Could be. Could be that someone else from the base had decided to use the back road tonight, maybe had already called in when they'd seen the crash—and learned that there should've been a third passenger, a certain dead man walking.

Maybe he was already being hunted.

He didn't move, straining to hear the movements of whoever had come in from the rain. For a few seconds, nothing—then he heard a soft tread, one step, then another. Moving away from him, toward the front of the car.

Billy leaned forward, carefully sliding his dog

tags under his collar so they wouldn't jingle, moving slowly, until he could just see around the edge of the aisle seat. Someone was stepping through the connecting door, thin, short—a girl, or a young man, maybe, dressed in a Kevlar vest and army green. He could just make out a few letters on the back of the vest, an *S,* a *T,* an *A*—and then he or she was gone.

S.T.A.R.S. Had they sent out a team looking for him? Couldn't be, not so fast—the jeep had crashed maybe an hour ago, tops, and the S.T.A.R.S. didn't have a military affiliation, they were a PD offshoot, no one would have called them in. It probably had to do with the dogs he saw, obviously some mutant feral pack; the S.T.A.R.S. usually dealt with the weird shit that local cops couldn't or wouldn't handle. Or maybe they'd come in to investigate whatever had gone down on the train.

Doesn't matter why, does it? They'll have guns, and if they figure out who you are, this taste of freedom will be your last. Get out of here. Now.

With man-eating dogs running around in the woods? Not without a weapon, no way. There had to be some kind of security on board, a rented uniform with a gun; he just had to look. It would be a risk, with a S.T.A.R.S. on board—but there was only one of them, after all. If he had to . . .

Billy shook his head. He'd seen his share of death in Special Forces. If it came down to it, here and

S.D. PERRY

now, he'd fight, or run. He wouldn't kill, not ever again. At least not one of the good guys.

Billy crawled to his feet, keeping low, the handcuffs dangling from his wrist. He'd look through the stuff in this car, first, then move away from the S.T.A.R.S. interloper, see what he could find. No point in having a confrontation if it could be avoided. He'd just—

Bam! Bam! Bam!

Three shots, from the car ahead. A pause, then three, four more . . . then nothing.

Apparently, not all the train cars were empty. The knot in his stomach tightened, but he didn't let it slow him down as he picked up the first briefcase he saw and started to dig.

The first train car was empty of life—but something very bad had occurred there, no question.

A crash? No, there's no structural damage . . . but so much blood!

Rebecca closed the door behind her, shutting out the thickening curtain of rain, and stared at the chaos around her. The cabin had been a nice one, all dark wood and expensive carpeting, the light fixtures antique, the wallpaper flocked. Now there were newspapers, suitcases, coats, bags open and spilled across the floor—it *looked* like there'd been a crash, and the drips and smears of blood that liberally dappled the cabin's walls and seats backed up the scenario. Except where were the passengers?

She stepped further into the train car, aiming the handgun up and down the aisle. There were a few low lights on, enough to see, but the shadows were deep. Nothing moved.

The back of the seat to her left was stained with blood. She reached out and touched the large splotch, then wiped her hand on her pants, grimacing. It was wet.

Lights are on, blood's fresh. Whatever happened, it happened recently. Lieutenant Billy, maybe? He was wanted for murder . . . Unless he had a gang with him, though, it didn't seem likely; the destruction was too widespread, too extreme, more like a natural disaster than some kind of hostage situation.

Or more like the forest murders.

She nodded inwardly, taking a deep breath. The killers must have struck again. The bodies that had been recovered had been torn apart, mutilated, and the crime scenes had probably looked exactly like this blood-spattered train car. She should get off now, radio the captain, call in the rest of the team. She started to turn back to the door—and hesitated.

I could secure the train first.

Ridiculous. It would be crazy to stay here by herself, stupid and dangerous. No one would expect her to check out a murder scene alone—assuming anyone *had* been murdered. For all she knew, there'd been a shooting or something, and the train had been evacuated.

No, that's stupid. There'd be cops all over the place, EMTs, helicopters, reporters. Whatever happened here, I'm the first one on the scene . . . and securing the scene is the first priority.

She couldn't help wondering what the guys might say when they saw she'd handled things herself. They'd stop calling her "kiddo," for one thing. At the very least, her rookie status would be behind her that much quicker. She could take a quick look around, nothing major, and if things seemed even the slightest bit dangerous, she'd call in the team, pronto.

She nodded to herself. Right. She could handle a look-see, no problem. A deep breath, and she started for the front of the car, carefully stepping through the scattered luggage. When she reached the connecting door, she braced herself and quickly stepped through, opening the second door before she lost her nerve.

Oh, no.

The first car had been bad, but here, there were people. Three, four—five that she could see from where she stood, and all of them obviously dead, faces ravaged by unknown claws, bodies drenched in dark wetness. A few were slumped in seats, as if they'd been brutally murdered where they'd been sitting. The smell of death was a palpable thing, like copper and feces, like rotting fruit on a hot day.

The door automatically closed behind her and she started, her heart beating fast, faintly aware that she was way out of her league, she needed to call for help—and then she heard the whispering, and realized that she wasn't alone.

She aimed her weapon at the empty aisle ahead, not sure where it was coming from, her heartbeat going double-time.

"Identify yourself!" she said, her voice firmer and more authoritative than she expected. The whispering continued, choking and distant, strangely muted in the otherwise silent car, like she imagined a crazed killer might sound, sitting and whispering to himself after a murder spree.

She was about to repeat herself when she saw the source of the whispering, halfway up the aisle on the floor. It was a tiny transistor radio, apparently tuned to an AM news station. She walked toward it, dazed by a sudden rush of relief; she was alone, after all.

She stopped in front of the radio, lowering her semi-automatic. There was a body in the window seat to her left, and after an initial glance, she avoided looking at it; the man's throat had been slashed, and his eyes had rolled back into his head. His gray face and tattered clothes were shining with viscous-looking fluids, making him look like a zombie from a bad horror movie.

She bent and picked the radio up, smirking at herself in spite of the fear that still coursed through her. Her "crazed killer" was a woman delivering a news report. The reception was bad, the tiny unit hissing static at every other sentence.

Okay, so she was an idiot. In any case, it was time to call Enrico, and Rebecca turned, thinking she'd get better reception if she stepped back outside, and the movement that came from the window seat was so slow and subtle that for a moment, she thought it was just the rain she was seeing. Then the movement groaned, a deep, low sound of misery, and she understood that it wasn't the rain at all.

The corpse had risen from his seat, and was moving toward her. His misshapen head lolled back and to the side, cruelly exposing the mauled flesh of his throat, and the moaning grew deeper, more yearning, as he stretched his arms in front of him, his ruined face dripping blood and slime.

She dropped the radio and took one stumbling step back, horrified. She'd been wrong, he wasn't dead, but he was obviously out of his mind with pain. She had to help him. *Not much in the medkit, there's morphine, though, gotta get him to lay down, oh, God, what* happened *here*—

The man shuffled closer, reaching for her, his eye

sockets filled with white, black drool spilling from his torn mouth—and in spite of what she knew was her duty, to do something to relieve his suffering, she reflexively took another step back. Duty was one thing, her instincts were telling her to run, to get away, that he meant to do her harm.

She turned, not sure what to do—and there were two more people standing in the aisle behind her, both as slack-faced and damaged as the white-eyed man, both moving toward her with the steady, staggering movements of horror movie monsters. The man in front wore a uniform, he was some kind of train attendant, his face gaunt, skull-like, and gray. Behind him, a man whose face had been partly torn away, revealing too many teeth on the right side of his mouth.

Rebecca shook her head, raising her weapon. Some kind of disease, a chemical spill, or something. They were sick, they had to be sick—except she knew better even as the three men moved closer, raising bony gray fingers, moaning with hunger. Maybe they *were* sick, but they were also about to attack her. She knew it as surely as she knew her own name.

Shoot! Do it!

"Stop!" she shouted, turning back to the white-eyed man, he was closer, too close, and if he was aware that she was pointing a handgun at him, he gave no sign. "I'll shoot!"

"Aaaahh," the monster rasped, grasping for her, baring dark teeth, and Rebecca fired.

Two, three shots, the rounds tearing into the discolored flesh, the first two hitting his chest, the third blowing a hole just above his right eye. With the third shot, the creature let out a mindless squeal, a sound of frustration rather than pain, and fell to the floor.

She spun again, praying that the sound of shots had stopped the other two, and saw that they were almost upon her, their eyes glazed, their moans eager. Her first shot hit the uniformed man in the throat, and as he reeled back, she aimed for the second man's leg. *Maybe I can just wound him, get him down*—

The uniformed man started forward again, his throat gurgling blood.

"God," she said, her voice small with shock, but they were still coming, she didn't have time to wonder, to think. She raised her aim and fired two, three more times, all head shots. Blood and flesh sprayed, torn. The two men went down.

Sudden silence, stillness, and Rebecca's wide gaze searched the car, her body thrumming with adrenaline. There were two, three more "corpses," but none of them moved.

What just happened? I thought they were dead.
They *were* dead. They were zombies.

No, there was no such thing. Rebecca checked to be sure there was another round in the chamber, doing it automatically as she struggled to understand. They weren't zombies, not like in the movies. If they'd truly been dead, the shots wouldn't have made them bleed like that; blood didn't pump if the heart wasn't beating.

But they only went down after the head shots. True. But that could still mean some sort of disease, maybe something that blocked pain receptors . . .

The forest murders. Rebecca felt her eyes widen even more, putting the pieces together. If there *had* been some kind of chemical spill or sickness, it might have affected any number of people up here in the woods, making them attack others. There'd been recent reports of wild, feral dogs, too—was it possible that the sickness was trans-species? Some of the victims had been partially eaten, bites made by human *and* animal jaws on at least two of the bodies.

She heard a soft movement, and stopped breathing. Back by the door she'd come through, a seated corpse seemed to slump lower in its seat. She watched it for what seemed an eternity, but it didn't move again, the only sound that of the rain outside. Corpse, or victim of some tragic circumstance? She didn't want to find out.

Rebecca backed away, stepping over the man with white eyes, now very much dead, deciding she'd try the door at the front of the car. She had to get off the train, tell the others what she'd found. Her head spun with what needed to happen next—the community would have to be alerted, a quarantine set up, right away. The federal government should get involved, too, the CDC or USAMRID or maybe the EPA, an agency with the power to close everything down, figure out what had happened. It would be a huge undertaking, but she could really contribute, really make a—

The corpse at the back of the car shifted again, its head settling against its chest, and all thoughts of saving Raccoon fled from her shocked mind. Rebecca turned and ran to the connecting door, sick with fear. All she wanted was out.

It didn't take too long to find a weapon, and as luck would have it, Billy was intimately familiar with the standard-issue MP handgun he found in a duffel bag stuffed under a seat. It was the same kind that his escort had carried. There was a spare clip and a half box of 9x19mm parabellum rounds, too, as well as a flip-top lighter, another handy device to have around; one never knew when fire might be necessary.

He loaded up, stuffing the clip into his belt and the extra rounds into his front pockets, wishing he had his fatigues on instead of civvies. Blue jeans weren't the best for carrying shit around. He started to look for a jacket, then decided against it; even with the rain it was a warm night, and slogging around in wet denim would be bad enough. The small pockets would have to do.

He stood at the door that led back into the woods, weapon in hand, telling himself that he needed to get gone—and yet not leaving. He hadn't heard anything from the S.T.A.R.S. kid since those seven shots. Only a few minutes had passed; if the kid was in trouble, it wasn't too late for him to step in and—

Are you crazy? his brain shouted at him. *Go! Run, you idiot!*

Right, of course. He had to leave. But he couldn't get the ring of those shots out of his head, and he'd spent too long as one of the good guys to turn his back on one of them, if they needed help. Besides, if the kid *was* dead, that would mean an extra weapon.

"Yeah, that's it," he mumbled, perfectly aware that he was searching for a more criminal-minded reason to justify his decision. There was no help for it; he had to go look.

With an internal groan, Billy turned away from the door, from freedom, moving instead to the front of the car. He stepped through the first door, hesitating a beat in the connecting joint before grasping the handle to the second, into the next car. The only sound was the rain outside, working its way into a real storm. As quietly as he could, he slid the second door open and stepped through.

The unmistakable smell hit him first. His jaw tightened as he surveyed the car, counting heads. Three in the aisle. Two up ahead on the right, and one directly to his left, slumped down in a seat. All of them dead.

The man in the road . . .

Billy frowned, realizing that any one of the corpses around him could have passed for the dork who'd stepped in front of the jeep, causing the crash. He'd only caught a glimpse of the guy, but remembered thinking that he'd looked sick. Maybe one of these people—but no, they'd been dead for days.

So what was the kid shooting at?

Billy moved closer to the nearest corpse, squatting next to it, taking in the wounds with a trained eye as he breathed shallowly through his mouth. The guy had been dead for awhile; part of his right cheek was missing, making him appear to grin widely up at Billy, and the edges of the torn tissue were rotting, black with decay. And yet there were one, two bullet holes in his brow, and a pool of very fresh blood surrounded his head and upper body like a red shadow. Billy touched the pool with the side of his hand, his frown deepening. It was warm. The next closest body, a train attendant, looked pretty much the same, only one of the wounds was in his throat.

He was no Einstein, but he wasn't entirely incapable of logic, either. The fresh blood could only mean that these people just *looked* dead. And the fact that they were now full of holes suggested that they'd tried to attack the lone S.T.A.R.S. member.

Which means I'd better be damned careful, he thought, rising to his feet. He looked back at the body in the seat now behind him, his gaze narrowing. Had the man moved, or was it a trick of the light? Either way, he'd just as soon be somewhere else.

He hurried up the aisle, stepping over corpses, trying to watch all of them at once and cursing his need to find the S.T.A.R.S. kid. If only he didn't have a goddamned *conscience,* he'd be long gone by now.

He slipped through the two doors, weapon ready as he entered the next car. It wasn't a passenger car, wasn't as nicely decorated; from the entrance, he could only see a short corridor that turned up ahead, and two closed doors to his right, a few windows opposite. He considered checking the rooms, aware that it would be the smartest move—turning your back to an unsecured area was a bad call—but he was starting to think that his conscience could go screw. He didn't want to secure the entire train, he just wanted to see that the kid was okay and then get the hell out.

And if said kid doesn't show up in the next couple of minutes, I'm deboarding anyhow. This sucks.

"Sucks" wasn't the word, it didn't begin to describe the low terror he felt in his gut—but he'd seen fear cripple the strongest men, and knew better than to dwell on thoughts of monsters and darkness. Better to laugh it off as a bad dream and get on with things.

He edged down the corridor, moving silently, sliding along the wall as the hall jagged right and then continued on, past an open door with a spill of cardboard boxes blocking the entrance. Storage room, probably. There were no bodies, at least, but a smell of rot hung in the air. The few unbroken windows he passed reflected a pale shadow of himself, only blackness and rain outside. He noted with dismay that some of the glass from the shattered panes was inside the car, scattered across the dark wood floor . . . Which suggested that someone had been trying to get *in,* not out. Creepy.

It looked like the corridor jagged left again up ahead, just past another closed door labeled CONDUCTOR'S OFFICE. He had to be near the front by now—

—and he saw a second pale shadow up ahead, reflected in a window, directly past the turn. He stopped, held very still, watched as the figure crouched down, his or her back to the corridor, oblivious to any threat from behind. If it was the S.T.A.R.S., he or she needed more training.

Billy took the last few steps and raised his weapon, moving in behind the crouched figure. He knew he should avoid a confrontation—the kid was obviously fine and dandy, and he had other places to be—but he also wanted to know what was happening, and this might be his only chance for information.

The S.T.A.R.S. member turned, saw Billy, and slowly, slowly stood up, facing him.

"Kid" isn't far off the mark, he thought, staring down into the wide, innocent eyes of a teenager, a girl. God, were they hiring out of high schools these days? She was small, at least a half foot shorter than he, and pretty—reddish-brown hair, slim, muscular build, even, delicate features. If she weighed more than a hundred pounds, he would have been surprised.

She'd been crouching in front of a dead man, his savaged body slouched in the corner next to the car's exit, and if she was surprised to see him, she hid it well.

"Billy," she said, her young voice clear and melodic, her words making him grit his teeth. "Lieutenant Coen."

Shit. Someone had found the jeep, after all.

He kept the gun raised, aimed directly at her right eye, playing it cool. "So. You seem to know me. Been fantasizing about me, have you?"

4 1

"You were the prisoner being transferred for execution," she said, her voice taking on a hard edge. "You were with those soldiers outside."

She thinks I did it, that I killed them, he thought. It was written all over her pixie face. He realized then that she probably didn't know a thing about what was going on, if she hadn't connected the walking-corpse-guys to what had happened to the jeep. And he saw no reason to disillusion her. She was trying to look tough, but he could see that he intimidated her. He could use it to get out of this.

"Uh-huh, I see," he said. "You're with S.T.A.R.S. . . . Well, no offense, honey, but your kind doesn't seem to want me around. So I'm afraid our little chat time is over."

He lowered his gun, then turned and walked away, his gait easy and unhurried—as though he wasn't the slightest bit concerned by her presence. He was counting on her obvious inexperience and fear of him to keep her from acting. It was a calculated risk, but he thought it would pay off.

He tucked his weapon into his belt at the small of his back and was halfway back down the corridor when he heard her jogging to catch up. Shit *shit*.

"Wait! You're under arrest!" she said firmly.

He turned to face her, and saw that she hadn't even unholstered her weapon. She was doing her damnedest to look fierce, but she couldn't pull it off.

If the situation had been less serious, any less bizarre, he would have smiled.

"No thanks, dollface. I've already worn the handcuffs," he said, holding up his left hand and jangling the hanging cuff. He turned and started away again.

"I could shoot, you know!" she called after him, but now there was an edge of desperation to her voice; he kept walking. She didn't follow, and a few seconds later, he was back through the first connecting door.

He opened the door to the car of dead passengers wearing a shaky grin, relieved. It was better this way, every man for himself, and all that—

—and he saw that the dead man who'd been slumped in his seat at the back was now standing, swaying, his one remaining eye fixed on Billy's position. With a moan of hunger, the creature shambled forward, reaching out with shredded fingers as though to feel his way to where Billy stood.

THREE

Rebecca watched as Billy stalked out of the train car, feeling impotent and very young. He didn't even look back, as though she wasn't worth worrying about.

And apparently I'm not, she thought, her shoulders sagging. She hadn't expected him to be so— well, scary. Big, muscular, with dark steely eyes and an intricate tribal tattoo covering his entire right arm, both arms bared by a thin cotton undershirt. He looked tough, and after her terrifying run-in with the walking near-dead, she hadn't been up to the task of taking him into custody.

Not to mention, he got the drop on you. She'd found a lone corpse at the front of the car, one of the train workers, and had seen what looked like a key grasped in one cold hand. Since the only other door out of the car was locked, she'd had to try for it—it was that, or go back through the passenger car. She'd been so involved in trying to retrieve the key without snapping the stiff fingers that she hadn't heard the convict approach, not until it was too late. Now, as she walked back to the front of the car, she saw that the locked door used a card reader, anyway. Great. So far, she was doing just great.

She turned and reached for her radio, ready to admit defeat. If she could get the team in fast enough, they'd handle Billy. More important, she wouldn't be alone with the knowledge that some kind of plague had hit Raccoon. It was funny, that nabbing a convicted killer was suddenly lower on the list of priorities . . .

Bam! Bam!

Before she'd even touched the transmitter button, she heard two rounds fired in the next car, the direction Billy had gone. She hesitated, not sure what to do—and in that instant, a window exploded behind her.

She spun, shards of glass flying, and saw a human figure falling to the floor.

"Edward!"

The mechanic didn't respond. Rebecca rushed to her teammate's side, quickly assessing his condition.

Besides a massive, open wound on his right shoulder, his face was gray with shock, his gaze bleary and unfocused. Every exposed part of his body was covered with contusions and abrasions.

"Are you all right?" she asked, ripping her medkit open, grabbing a thick gauze patch. She tore the package apart, applied it to his shoulder, realizing with a sinking sensation that it might not do much good; from the massive amount of blood drenching his shirt, his subclavian had likely been severed. She was astounded that he was still alive, let alone that he'd had the strength to jump through a window. "What happened?"

Edward rolled his head towards her, blinking slowly. His voice was taut with pain. "Worse than . . . We can't . . ."

She held the bandage firmly, but it was already soaked through. He needed a hospital, ASAP, or he wasn't going to make it.

Edward's voice was getting weaker. "You must be careful, Rebecca," he slurred. ". . . forest is full of zombies . . . and monsters . . ."

She started to tell him not to talk any more, to conserve his energy—when more glass exploded, slivers of it raining over them, the window just to their left shattering. One, two giant dark shapes leaped through the broken pane, one disappearing around a jag in the corridor, the other turning in their direction.

Zombies and monsters.

A dog, it was a big dog, but like no dog she'd ever seen before. It might have been a Doberman, once—but as it bared dripping teeth at her, flaps of skin and muscle hanging from its haunches, she realized that it, too, had been infected by whatever disease had struck the train's passengers. It didn't just look dead, it looked *destroyed,* its eyes filmed with red, its body like some mad patchwork quilt of wet fur and bloody tissue.

Edward wouldn't be able to protect himself. Rebecca slowly rose and took a step back from the dying mechanic, gun in hand, though she couldn't remember drawing it. She could hear the second dog panting farther along the corridor, out of sight.

She aimed for the animal's left eye, really understanding the true horror of the disease, whatever it was, for the first time. Her conflict with the near-dead passengers had been terrible, but so shocking she'd hardly had time to consider what it all meant. Now, looking at the stiff-legged, monstrous beast in front of her, its growl rising into a hellish whine of hunger, she remembered her childhood pet, a shaggy black lab mix named Donner, remembered how much she'd loved him—and understood that this had probably been someone's pet, once, too. Just as those people she'd shot had once been human, had laughed and cried and come from families that would miss them, that would be destroyed by their loss. Disease, chemical spill, or attack, whatever had caused all this, it was an abomination.

The understanding flashed through her mind in an instant, and was gone. The dog tensed its shredded flanks, preparing to leap at her, and Rebecca squeezed the trigger, the nine-millimeter rocking in her hands, the blast of sound deafening in the small space. The dog collapsed.

Rebecca pivoted, aiming at the bit of corridor she could see, waiting for the second to appear. She didn't have to wait long.

With a snarl, the animal leaped around the corner, its jaws wide. Rebecca fired, the shot hitting its chest, staggering the dog back with a high whine of pain—but it was still on its feet. It shook itself as though shaking off water, growling, readying to come at her again even as dark, ichorous blood poured from its wound.

Should have killed it, that should have knocked it flat!

Just like the people in the passenger car, it seemed that only a head shot would take it down. She raised her aim and fired again, this time hitting the center of its bullet-shaped skull. The dog fell, spasmed once, and went still.

There could be more of them. She lowered the gun slightly, turning toward the broken windows and trying to see through the darkness and rain, straining to hear anything besides the storm. After a few beats she gave up, kneeling next to Edward again, reaching into her pack for a fresh bandage—

—and stopped, staring at her teammate. The steady pump of blood from his shoulder wound was no more. She quickly felt for a pulse below his left ear, felt nothing at all. Edward gazed at the floor with half open eyes, dead.

"I'm sorry," she whispered, sitting back on her heels. It seemed inconceivable that he was gone, that he'd died in the short time she'd been shooting at the dog-things, and a wash of guilt swept over her. If she'd been faster, if she'd packed his wound better . . .

. . . *But you didn't, and the longer you sit here feeling bad about it, the more likely it is that you'll end up joining him. Get moving.*

Rebecca felt new guilt at the insensitive thought, but a glance at the open windows got her on her feet. She'd have to assess her culpability later, when it was safe to do so.

Her radio beeped. She grabbed it, backing away from the windows, from poor Edward.

Reception was bad, but she could tell it was Enrico. She held the speaker to her ear, hugely relieved to hear the captain's strong voice in between bursts of static.

". . . you copy? . . . more information on . . . Coen . . ."

Rebecca reluctantly stepped closer to the windows, hoping to hear better, but the static barely lifted.

". . . institutionalized . . . killed at least twenty-three people . . . careful . . ."

What? Rebecca pressed the transmit button. "Enrico, this is Rebecca! Do you read me? Over."

A wave of static.

"Captain! S.T.A.R.S. Bravo, do you copy?"

Long seconds of more static. She'd lost the signal. Rebecca put the radio back on her belt. She had to get to the 'copter, tell the others about Edward, about Billy and the train and the terrible danger they were all facing. She changed clips for the nine-millimeter, taking a moment to reload the half spent one. With a final sorrowful look at her fallen teammate, she stepped over a dog body, doing her best to avoid slipping in the pool of blood surrounding it, and started back toward the passenger car.

Although she knew she should be eager to run across the missing convict, to arrest him, she hoped she wouldn't see Billy again. Edward's death, the dogs . . . She felt unsteady, incapable of taking charge. And twenty-three people? She shuddered, amazed that he hadn't killed her when he'd had the chance.

In the passenger car, she saw the result of the two

shots she'd heard earlier. The disease victim she'd thought had moved, but hadn't been sure about . . . It seemed he'd been alive, after all. He must have tried to attack Billy, the way the others had gone after her. She paused at the door back to the car she'd originally come through, looking over the decayed bodies of the people she'd killed. If Edward was right, if the woods were full of these things, she was going to have to move fast—

—and maybe Billy didn't kill those marines.

Rebecca blinked. It hadn't occurred to her earlier, but the jeep may have been attacked, allowing Billy to escape—forcing him to run, in fact. It seemed likely. The two dead men had been mauled, not just shot; the dogs could have done it.

She shook her head. It didn't matter. He was a killer, either way, and if she wasn't up to the job of apprehending him, she'd better go get someone who could. As serious as the unknown sickness was, they couldn't just let Coen run.

She left the passenger car behind, hurrying through the empty car to the side door, hoping that the others were all back at the helicopter, safe. She reached for the handle, lifted it. She wasn't sure how to break the news about Edward, that was going to be rough—

Rebecca frowned, pushing at the sliding door, which was refusing to slide. She tried the handle again, then again . . . and then kicked the door, cursing silently. It was stuck—or Billy had locked it, maybe to keep her from following him.

"Damn." She chewed at her lower lip, remembering that key in the dead worker's hand. She hadn't managed to pull it free, and then had forgotten about it after her run-in with Billy, not to mention Edward and the dogs . . . But then, who needed keys? She could just as easily crawl out through one of the broken windows, no big deal—

She heard a sound, a door closing, and looked to her left, toward the back of the train. Someone was moving around in the next car over. Another sick passenger, probably. Or perhaps Billy *was* still on board. Either way, she was ready to get off, and she had her choice of windows to exit.

Unless . . . it's someone else back there. Someone who needs help.

It could even be another of the S.T.A.R.S., and now that she'd thought of it, she felt duty-bound to take a look, sensible or not. She walked quickly to the end of the empty car, readying herself for whatever would come next. It didn't seem possible that anything weirder could happen tonight—but then, most of what had already happened didn't seem possible. She wanted to be prepared for anything.

She opened the door to the next car and took it in with a sweep of the nine-millimeter, vastly relieved to find it empty and blood-free. There were stairs going up on the left, a door straight ahead. That must have been the door she'd heard closing . . .

. . . And now it opened, and out walked Billy Coen.

Billy stopped, stared at the girl, at the weapon in her hand—and was glad. That she was still alive, that she had a gun and apparently knew how to use it. After what he'd just learned, having a partner might be his only chance to survive.

"This is bad," he said, and could see that she knew he wasn't referring to the gun in his face. She didn't answer, only watched him steadily, her nine-millimeter unwavering, and he raised his hands, understanding that game time was over. The dangling handcuff slapped his wrist.

"Those people—the ones you had to kill—they were sick," he said. "One of them tried to bite me. I shot him, and found a notebook in his jacket. May I—?"

He started to lower one of his hands, to reach for his back pocket.

"No! Keep your hands up!" she said, jerking the weapon. She still seemed scared, but was apparently prepared to arrest him.

"Okay, fine," he said. "You get it. It's in my right back pocket."

"You're kidding, right? I'm not coming near you."

Billy sighed. "It's important, some kind of a diary. It doesn't make a lot of sense, something about an investigation into a lab that's been abandoned or destroyed—but it also talks about a bunch of murders that have happened around here, and the possibility that a virus has been released. Something called T-virus."

He saw a spark of interest, but she was playing it safe. "I'll read it after you put that handcuff back on," she said.

He shook his head. "Whatever's happening, it's dangerous. Someone locked all the exits, have you noticed? Why don't we cooperate, until we can get out of this?"

"Cooperate?" Her eyebrows rose. "With *you?*"

He stepped closer, lowering his hands, ignoring the gun in his face. "Listen, little girl—if you haven't noticed, there's some pretty freaked out shit on this train. I, for one, want to get out of here, and we don't stand a chance of doing it alone."

She didn't lower the gun. "You expect me to trust you? I don't need your help, I can handle this on my own. And don't call me little girl."

She was starting to piss him off, but he reined it in. He didn't need her as an enemy. "All right, Miss Do-It-Yourself," he said. "What should I call you?"

"The name is Rebecca Chambers," she said. "That's *Officer* Chambers to you."

"Well then, Rebecca, why don't you tell me your plan of action?" he asked. "You gonna arrest me? Great, do it. Call the whole force in, and tell 'em to bring heavy artillery. We can wait here for them."

For the first time, she seemed to falter. "Radio's out," she said.

Hell. "How'd you get here?" he asked. "Air or ground? How close is your transport?"

"We came in by 'copter, but . . . there was a malfunction," she said. "Not that it's any of your business. Put the cuff back on. My team is waiting outside."

Billy lowered his hands, slowly. "How far? Are you sure they're still around?"

The girl scowled. "This isn't twenty questions, Lieutenant. I'm taking you out of here. Turn around and face the wall."

"No." Billy crossed his arms. "Shoot me if you have to, but there's no way I'm giving up my weapon or letting you cuff me."

High color flared in her cheeks. "You'll do what I tell you, or I'll—"

Crash!

Windows breaking, in the upstairs compartment. Billy and Rebecca both looked up, then at each other. A few seconds later, they heard what sounded like heavy footsteps overhead, slow and even . . . Then nothing at all.

"Dining room," Billy said. "And it was empty a few minutes ago."

Rebecca studied him for a moment, then lowered her weapon slightly. She moved to the foot of the stairs and looked up, her youthful face set with a determined expression. "Wait here," she said. "I'll check it out."

Billy almost smiled. He'd been in Special Forces for seven years, had learned how to shoot quite probably before she was out of grade school—and *she* was going to protect *him?*

"I thought you didn't trust me," he said. "What's to stop me from climbing out one of the windows, making my escape?"

The girl *did* smile, a small and cold affair. "It's dangerous, remember? You don't stand a chance of doing it alone."

Before he could come up with something properly snappy, she had turned her back and walked up the stairs, apparently determined to prove to him that she was a competent authority figure. Dumb kid; with all that was going on, proving herself shouldn't have been her top priority. He knew he should probably follow her, keep her from getting herself killed, but he wanted a minute to think. He watched as she reached the top of the stairs and disappeared around a corner, not looking back.

Like the song says, should I stay or should I go? Rebecca wanted to arrest him, but that also meant she'd have to keep him alive. And she needed his help, no question; she was too inexperienced to be out here by herself.

So who died and appointed you her personal savior? When are you gonna get it? You're not one of the good guys anymore, remember?

Running still wasn't out of the question, but he no longer felt so sure of his chances. If he'd needed more proof that the woods were hazardous, the notebook he'd found, the pocket journal of the man who'd attacked him, was more than enough. He pulled it out, flipping to the last few entries, the ones that had caught his eye.

July 14th. We heard today about the Arklay lab . . . and we're being sent in to check it out next week. Some of the others are worried about the conditions, about what might be left, but like the boss says, someone's got to take the first look. Might as well be us . . .

The writer went on to talk about his girlfriend, who'd be angry that he was leaving town. Billy skipped ahead, skimming the pages for what he'd read before.

July 16th . . . There's still so much we don't know about responses to the T-virus. Depending on the species and environment, only minute doses of T bring about remarkable changes in size, aggressive behavior, and brain development . . . in animals, anyway. Nothing's immune. But until the effects can be better controlled, the company's playing with fire.

Billy turned a page.

July 19th. The day is finally approaching . . . I'm more anxious than I thought I'd be. The Raccoon City newspapers and TV stations have been reporting bizarre murders in the suburbs. It can't be the virus. Can it? If it is . . . No. I can't think of that now. I have to concentrate on the investigation, make sure it goes smoothly.

Changes in size, aggressive behavior, brain development. Like, say, in a dog? And that bit about "in animals, anyway." What did this T-virus to do humans? Billy was willing to bet he'd already seen the results.

"Turns 'em into zombies," he muttered. Or as good as zombies, anyway. The one he'd shot had definitely been looking for lunch. What was it that cannibals called humans? Long pig, that was it. That walking mess had wanted some long pig, no question.

Woods full of cannibals and monsters . . . he'd take his chances with the girl. She'd held her own so far, had killed at least three of those passengers and had managed to hang on to her sanity. He'd stay with her until they got out of this—and then he'd work out an escape before the rest of her team moved in, assuming there was any of her team left—

A girl, *the* girl screamed from overhead, a sound of pure terror. Billy grabbed his weapon and bolted up the stairs, two at a time, hoping he hadn't waited too long to make up his mind.

At the top of the stairs was a slight curve, then a door. Rebecca opened it slowly, carefully, with the muzzle of the handgun, and stepped inside.

A thin, acrid haze of smoke greeted her, and the low flicker of fire, making shadows dance on the walls. It was a dining car, like Billy had said, and had once been beautiful, the tables covered in fine linen, the windows draped with cream-colored curtains. Now it was trashed, plates and broken glass everywhere, tables overturned, the linens soaked with spilled wine and blood . . . And near the back, a lone figure sat hunched over a table, the hem of the tablecloth burning, the flames licking upward. Rebecca saw a small oil lamp smashed in front of the table, the cause of the fire. The fire was still small, but it might not be for long.

The man at the table was very still—and as Rebecca walked closer, she saw that he wasn't like the passengers below, wasn't infected by what Billy had suggested was the T-virus. He was an older, distinguished-looking man in a brown suit, his white hair slicked back, his head bent over his chest as though he'd nodded off during dinner.

Heart attack? Or had he passed out? It didn't seem likely that he'd broken a second-story window and climbed inside, but as far as she could tell, there was no one else in the room, no one else who could have made those heavy footsteps they'd heard.

Rebecca cleared her throat as she moved toward him. "Excuse me," she said, stopping next to the table, noticing that his face and hands were wet, gleaming slightly in the firelight. "Sir?"

No response—but he was breathing; she could see his chest moving. She leaned in, put her hand on his shoulder. "Sir?"

He started to raise his head, turning his face toward her—and there was a sick, wet sound, like lips smacking over something slimy, and the man's head slid from his torso and toppled to the floor.

The wet sound got louder, the decapitated body

starting to shake, to bubble with movement, as though filled with living things. Rebecca stumbled backward, letting out a scream as the man's body slid apart like badly stacked blocks, great pieces of it falling to the floor. When the pieces hit, they disintegrated, the cloth of the suit changing color, turning black, becoming many things, each the size of a fist.

Slugs they're like slugs—

Slugs with rows of tiny teeth, not slugs at all but leeches, fat and round and somehow able to mimic a man, even the man's clothes . . . *Not possible, this can't be happening!*

She stumbled back farther, sick with terror as the individual creatures came together once more, melding into one another, the mass of abnormal, bloated things growing into a glistening tower of darkness. They reformed, took shape and color—and again became the old man she'd seen sitting at the table. She stared in shock, in disbelief. Even knowing that he was made up of hundreds, perhaps thousands of the disgusting things, she couldn't see the spaces between them, wouldn't have known that it wasn't a man except that she'd seen it form for herself. The shade of the suit, the shape and color of the body— the only clue that it wasn't a man was the strangely shining quality of its skin and clothes.

It cocked its left arm back as though about to pitch a baseball, and then snapped it forward. The arm elongated, stretched impossibly. Rebecca was at least five meters away, but the glistening wet hand swatted at the air only centimeters from her face. She tripped over her own feet in her hurry to get away, falling to the floor as the arm snapped back into place—then cocked backward, ready to strike again.

Gun, stupid, shoot!

She jerked the weapon up and fired, the first two shots going wild, the third and fourth disappearing into the thing's lurching body. She could see the not-flesh ripple when the bullets hit, the suit and the body beneath it undulating slightly, as though she were seeing it through heat waves off of asphalt on a summer day. The creature barely hesitated before whipping its arm toward her once more. She dodged, but the hand made contact, slapping against her left cheek. She screamed again, more from the feel of the hand than the strength of the blow—it was cold and slimy and rough, like sharkskin dipped in pond scum—and before it withdrew, it slapped at her again, this time knocking the nine-millimeter from her hand. The weapon skittered across the floor, ending up beneath one of the tables. The old man–creature took another oddly lurching step, was now close enough that its next blow likely wouldn't be so easily evaded, and Rebecca just had time to think that she was dead—

—and *bam-bam-bam,* the creature was staggering back, and someone was firing again and again,
the unexpected sound making her cringe as she staggered to her feet. The first few shots disappeared
into its form like before, but the shooter kept at it,
finding the monster's aged and shining face, its
shining eyes. Dark liquid flew from sudden openings in the collective, leeches blowing to pieces, and
on the sixth or seventh shot, the man-thing began to
melt back into its component parts, the small, black
animals slithering toward the broken windows as
they hit the floor.

Rebecca looked back at the door and saw Billy
Coen standing there in a classic shooter's position,
both hands on his weapon, his gaze fixed on the
monstrosity in front of them as it finished its silent
collapse, becoming many once more. The leeches
continued to make for the windows, sliding on trails
of slime over the debris-littered floor and up the
stained walls, slipping effortlessly over the jagged
edges of glass and into the storming night. They had
finished their attack, it seemed.

A strange, high singing drifted in over the sound
of the rain. Still in shock, Rebecca walked to the
window, carefully avoiding the remaining leeches as
they streamed out of the car, retrieving her weapon
before looking out to find the source of the singing.
Billy joined her, making no effort to step over the

strange creatures; several popped wetly beneath his boot heels.

In a flash of lightning, they saw him. Standing on a low hill west of the train, a lone figure—male, from his height, from the width of the shoulders—raised long arms, a gesture of welcome, and sang in a surprisingly sweet soprano, his voice young and rich and strong. Latin, like something from church. As if that weren't bizarre enough, he seemed to be standing in a low, shallow lake, the ground rippling slightly all around him. It was too dark to see well, only deep shadow and silhouette marking the lonely singer.

"Oh, Christ," Billy said. "Look at that."

Rebecca felt the hairs on the back of her neck prickle, her mouth turning down in a grimace of disgust. There was no lake. The ground was covered with leeches, thousands of them, all moving toward the singing young man. She could see the hem of his long coat or robe flapping as the creatures flowed upward, disappearing beneath it.

"Who *is* that guy?" Billy asked, and Rebecca shook her head. Maybe like the old man, made from the creatures—

The train lurched suddenly. A rising, heavy mechanical sound filled the car, the floor vibrating beneath their feet—and then the train was moving, slowly at first, quickly picking up speed.

She looked at Billy, saw the same confused surprise on his face that she knew she wore, and for the first time, felt something besides angry disdain for the criminal. He was stuck in this—this nightmare, same as she was. *And he did just save my life . . .*

"Still handling things yourself?" he asked, smirking, and she felt the tenuous bond between them disappear. Before she could say anything, though, he seemed to realize that his passive-aggressive stab at humor wasn't what the situation called for.

"I think we could both use a little help here," he said. "How about it? Just until we're out of this, all right?"

Rebecca thought about the viral victims she'd seen, those she'd killed, about what Edward had said, that the woods were full of zombies and monsters. She thought about the man made of leeches, and their strange, singing master out in the rain, and finally about the fact that someone, or some *thing* had started the train. Even if Enrico and the rest of the team were still alive, they were falling farther and farther away by the minute.

"Yeah, okay," she said, and though his grim and arrogant demeanor didn't change, she thought that Billy was relieved. And she knew that she was.

FOUR

The solitary figure on the hill watched as the train gathered speed and disappeared into the storm, his heart full of the song that spilled from his lips, that rang so sweetly through the wild air, calling his minions back to him. They had done well, readying the train for the inevitable cleanup crew as soon as the sun had gone down, leading most of the infected away through the woods, locking the doors, powering the engine; he wanted the leeches to feed, not the virus carriers, and once the Umbrella team boarded, there would be no escape. The rain washed over the many as they crept up the hill, beckoned by his voice, by his desires.

He received them with a smile as he finished his

song. All was going as well as he might have wished. After so long a wait, it wouldn't be long, now. He would fulfill his dream; he would become Umbrella's nightmare, and then the world's.

"We need to stop this train, first thing," Rebecca said.

Billy nodded. "Any suggestions?"

"We split up," she said calmly. Surprisingly calmly, considering what she'd just been through. "The car at the front of the train is locked—where we met? We need to get that door open, to get to the engine."

"So, we shoot the lock," Billy said.

Rebecca shook her head. "Magnetic card reader. We have to find a key card."

"I saw a conductor's office—"

"Locked," Rebecca said. "We'll have to dig up one ourselves."

"That could take awhile," Billy said. "We should stick together."

"It'll take us twice as long. And I'd rather get off this thing before it ends up wherever it's going."

As much as he didn't want to wander the train alone, didn't want *her* to wander it alone, he couldn't argue with the logic.

"I'll start at the back, work forward," she said. "You take the second floor. We'll meet at the front."

Bossy little thing, aren't you? he thought, but kept it to himself. At some point in the not-too-distant future, she might be the only thing keeping him from becoming somebody's lunch.

"And I *will* shoot you if you try anything funny," she added. Billy started to snap back at her, then saw the shine in her eyes. She wasn't serious. Not entirely.

She nodded at his weapon. "You need ammo for that thing?"

"I'm good," he said. "You?"

Another nod, and she started for the door. When she reached it, she turned back.

"Thanks," she said, motioning vaguely toward the back of the car. "I owe you."

Before he could answer, she was gone. Billy stared after her a moment, somewhat amazed by her willingness to face the train's dangers on her own. Had he been so brave when he was her age?

It's called "denial of mortality" when you're that young, he thought. Yeah, he'd thought he'd live forever then, too. Being sentenced to death made one take a slightly different view on things.

He spent a brief moment checking the dining car, scowling at the smashed and liquid remains of a few dozen leech-things as he hurriedly checked behind the small bar, beneath the tables. There was a locked door at the front of the room, but a swift kick and a glance showed him an empty service cabin with a hole in the roof. He didn't linger, figuring their best bet would be searching the bodies of the train workers, anyway.

He headed down the stairs, pausing at the bottom a moment, looking toward the rear of the train before continuing on. Rebecca Chambers seemed capable of taking care of herself; better if he watched his own ass.

Back through the double doors, through the first passenger car, still empty, and a deep breath before heading into the second. A quick look to make sure there wasn't anyone walking around and he headed up the stairs, not wanting to look at the body of the man he'd killed. He'd killed before, but it was never something you got used to, not if you had a conscience.

The smell hit him before he reached the second floor and he slowed, breathing shallowly. Like sea water and rot. When he got to the top, he saw the source and swallowed back bile.

Now we know where they came from.

He'd stepped onto a landing at the top of the stairs, one that turned into a corridor to his immediate right, turning right again a few meters ahead— and from floor to ceiling, the corner of the landing to his left was webbed with what appeared to be hundreds of empty egg sacs, creating something like a spider's nest—only these sacs were black and wet, shining in the low light of a half-buried wall sconce. They swayed slightly as the train rocked back and forth on the track, making them appear almost alive. At least they were empty. He hoped to God he wouldn't run into whatever had laid them.

He edged away from the webbed corner, stepping on strings of the glistening matter that spread across the hall's fine carpet, vaguely wondering if the jeep accident had been such a blessing, after all. He didn't want to die in any manner, but a nice, clean firing squad beat the shit out of being devoured by shape-changing leeches.

Knock it off, soldier. Be where you are.

Right. He walked the corridor, relaxing slightly once he realized it was empty. There were two closed cabin doors, one on each side of the narrow passage, each marked by a number. From that and the hall's luxurious décor, he guessed they were private cabins. It was a good guess. He pushed open the first door, 102, and found a small bedroom, well-appointed and thankfully free of blood and bodies. Unfortunately, there wasn't much else, either, though he did find a clutter of personal belongings in the tiny closet. There were papers, a clutch of photographs, a jewelry box. He opened the box, revealing a silver ring, unusual in design; it looked like a single part of one of those interlocking ring sets, notched and warped in a distinct pattern . . . And since he wasn't jewelry shopping, he put it back, heading out to the next cabin.

When he opened the door to 101, he felt a rush of hope. There, lying on the floor like a gift, was a shotgun. Billy scooped it up and cracked it, his hope turning to a guarded happiness. It was a Western, over-under, loaded with two twelve-gauge shells. Further searching turned up another handful of shells, though no key card.

Magnetic lock or no, this'll probably open that door, he thought, comforted by the weight of the heavy weapon as he stuffed the shells into his front pocket. He was tempted to go find Rebecca immediately, but decided he might as well finish what he'd started. There was a door at the end of the hall, presumably leading to the next car's second floor, and it would lead him closer to the front of the train, anyway—the sooner to reunite with the kid. He wasn't scared to be on his own, it wasn't that, and it wasn't even concern for Rebecca, though that was there, too—it was too many years spent in service. If he'd learned anything, it was that being alone in combat was the worst way to be.

The door was unlocked, and opened into an empty lounge car, an extremely snazzy one. There was a polished wooden bar to his right, well stocked, and small, elegant tables lined either wall, leaving the wide, expensively carpeted floor open beneath low-hanging chandeliers. Like the last car, no blood or bodies. Billy checked the counters behind the bar, then headed for the door at the far end, feeling strangely ill at ease crossing the open space. He clutched the heavy shotgun firmly.

When he was almost across the room, something crashed onto the roof.

The sound was thunderous, huge, the impact so strong that a chandelier back by the bar hit the floor, the glass globes shattering. The train car rocked on its rails, causing him to stumble, almost fall.

He kept his feet, turning to look. Where the chandelier had fallen, the roof was actually indented, the thick metal twisted out of shape—and as he watched, one, two giant *things* pierced through, about two meters apart, one after the other.

Billy stared, not sure what he was seeing. Big, pointed cylindrical, each piercing piece appeared to be bisected, split down the middle. They looked like . . . claws?

His gut knotted. That was exactly what they were, like a giant crab's or scorpion's claws, and as he watched, they both opened, revealing thickly serrated edges. The huge pincers turned inward and up, began to actually saw through the steel roof, the sound of ripping metal like a high scream.

He'd seen enough. He turned and ran the last few

meters to the door out, aware that he'd broken out in a cold sweat. Behind him, the scream of tortured metal went on and on, and he grabbed the handle, jerked—

—and it was locked. Of course.

He spun back just in time to see the owner of the massive pincers jump down through the jagged entrance it had made, blocking the only other means of escape.

Rebecca had just decided the last car was safe when the dog attacked.

After leaving Billy, she'd made her way through a kitchen area in the last car, one awash in blood and fallen cookware, but otherwise empty. She was starting to wonder if some of the passengers and crew might have gotten off, perhaps when the train had first been attacked. There was a lot of blood around for so few bodies. Considering the state of the few passengers she'd run into, maybe that was for the best.

Her feet skidded through a puddle of cooking oil as she surveyed the kitchen, but her search was otherwise uneventful. The door to the rest of the car—presumably a storage area of some kind—was locked, but there was a crawl space that ran beneath the floor, with a covering she managed to pry up without too much trouble. She wasn't happy about having to crawl into a dark hole, but it was a short tunnel, just a couple of meters. Besides, she'd told Billy she would start at the back of the train, and she meant to be thorough. Doing a decent job was something to hold on to in the midst of such madness. The virus victims were bad enough, and that man made out of leeches . . .

. . . *Don't think about it. Find the keycard, stop the train, go get some real help. Someone besides a convicted killer, thank you very much.* Billy was her only port in the storm, so to speak, and he'd certainly saved her ass, but trusting him any further than she absolutely had to would be idiotic.

She'd been right about the next compartment. After a thankfully brief claustrophobic crawl, she stood up in a storage space, barely lit by a single hanging bulb. There were boxes and bins along the walls, mostly hidden in deep shadow. She swept the darkness with her weapon. Nothing moved but the train itself, rocking along the track.

At the back of the compartment was a door with a window in it. Rebecca stepped closer, nine-millimeter extended, saw darkness and movement on the other side, the sound of the train louder, and realized she was actually in the last car, looking out over the track. She felt a flutter of something like relief, just knowing that the world still existed out there—and that if worse came to worst, she could always jump. The train was going pretty fast, but it was an option.

Click.

She spun at the soft sound behind her, heart hammering, aiming at nothing. The train kept rolling along, the shadows pitching and swaying, the sound not repeated. After a tense moment, she took a deep breath, blew it out. Probably one of the boxes shifting. Like the rest of this car—well, the first floor, anyway—the storage compartment seemed to be safe. She doubted there'd be a keycard floating around, but at least she could say she'd looked—

—*click. Click. Click-click-click.*

Rebecca froze. The sound was *right next to her,* and she knew what it was, anyone who'd ever had a dog would know: the tick of toenails on a hard surface. She slowly turned her head to the right, to where she now saw there were a couple of dog carriers, both with their doors standing open. And emerging from the shadows behind the closest—

It all happened fast. With a vicious snarl, the dog leaped. She had time to register that it was like the others she'd seen—huge, infected, damaged—and then her right foot came up, the action reflexive. She kicked out, hard, and caught one side of the creature's barrel chest with her heel. With a horrible wet tearing sound, she heard as well as felt a sizable flap of the animal's chest slough away, the skin sliding off the graying muscle, the wet and matted fur sticking to the bottom of her oily shoe.

Incredibly, the dog ignored the wound and kept coming, its jaws wide and dripping. It would have her before she could get the gun up, she knew it, she could already feel the teeth clamping on her arm, and she also knew that a bite from this dog would kill her, would turn her into one of the walking near-dead—

—and before the teeth actually touched, her other foot, slick with oil, skidded out from beneath her. Rebecca hit the floor, banging her hip, and the dog flew overhead, a smell like rotten meat washing over her. It actually stepped on her, one back paw smearing dirt on her left shoulder as it bounded over, the momentum of its lunge carrying it past.

The wildly lucky fall had only bought her a second. She rolled onto her stomach, extended her arm and fired, catching the animal as it turned to lunge again. The first shot went high; the second found its mark, just below the poor beast's left eye.

The dog sagged to the floor, dead before it had stopped moving. Blood began to spread around the fallen dog, and Rebecca scrambled away, pushing herself to her feet. Beyond the very basics, virology wasn't her specialty, but she was willing to bet that the dog's blood was hot, highly infective, and she wasn't interested in catching whatever was going around. This wasn't a common head cold.

Assuming this is *a virus,* she thought, staring down at the decayed mess that had been a canine. It made as much sense as anything else, the mysterious T-virus Billy had talked about. How had it spread? What was the rate of toxicity, how quickly did it amplify once inside a host body?

She scraped the sole of her shoe against one of the kennels, hoping that she'd be able to erase that wet ripping sound from her memory as easily—and saw something glitter from the shadows. She leaned down, picked up a small gold ring, notched in an unusual design. It didn't appear to be real gold, was probably worthless, but it was pretty. And she was lucky to be standing there looking at it, all things considered.

"Which makes this a lucky ring," she said, and slipped in on her left index finger. It was very nearly a perfect fit.

The ring was all she found. There was no keycard lying around, nothing useful. She stepped out onto the back platform for a moment and was instantly drenched. The storm was torrential, and the train was moving much too quickly to consider jumping. Her hopes soared briefly when she saw a panel labeled EMERGENCY BRAKE LINE, but a few taps at the controls proved it to be powerless. So much for emergencies.

She went back inside, pushing her wet hair off

her forehead. Time to head forward, try searching the bodies of the men that she and Billy had killed. As distasteful as the thought was, there wasn't much of an alternative. They didn't know if anyone was driving the train, or if it was a runaway; either way, they needed to get control.

She looked back at the dog one more time before leaving—by the door, this time—thinking of how lucky she'd been, how easily she could have been bitten or mauled to death. No way would she let her guard down again; she only hoped Billy was having better luck.

Christ on a cross.

Billy stared, his mouth hanging open, his mind numb with the impossibility of the thing not ten meters in front of him.

It might have looked something like a scorpion, if scorpions grew as big as sports cars. The monster that fell through the train's roof was insectile, maybe three meters long, with a pair of giant, armored claws snapping around its flat face, a long, bloated tail that curved up over its back, that ended in a curled stinger bigger than Billy's head. There were multiple legs, but Billy wasn't in a counting mood—not with the thing moving toward him, emitting a sound like an overheated engine as its massive, jointed legs pounded across the floor. Rain poured down from the hole in the roof, making the scene all the more hellish, the creature emerging from the wet haze like a bad dream.

No time to think. Billy shouldered and cocked the hunting gun and aimed for the thing's low, flat skull. Between the motion of the train and the monstrosity's loping scrabble, it took him a few seconds to be sure of the shot, a few seconds that seemed like an eternity. The creature scrabbled closer, its stiffly haired feet gouging up flaps of the expensive carpet with each rumbling step.

Billy squeezed, *boom,* the shotgun slapping against his shoulder hard enough to bruise. A hit, and the thing screeched, a splash of milky fluid erupting from the plated skull. He didn't pause to assess damage, only re-aimed and fired again, *boom.*

The thing was screeching ever louder, but still coming. Billy broke the shotgun, jerked the empty shells out, dug for more. He fumbled, shells spilling to the carpet, the shrieking monster closing the distance fast, too fast.

There was a single shell left in his pocket. He got it out, jammed it home and brought the rifle up to his hip . . . , *This better be the one—*

The shot hit the monster square in the center of its dark, ugly face, only a meter from where Billy stood, close enough that he felt the heat of gunpowder residue hitting his bare skin, embedding there. Its screech died as a large, jagged chunk of exoskeleton blew out the back of its head, splattering the spasming tail with blood and brain matter. It shivered all over, its huge claws whipping outward, opening and closing, its stinger jabbing at air. With a final gurgling cry, it sank to the floor, seeming to deflate as its heavy claws, its body, came to rest.

The smell of it, like dirt and hot, sour grease was nearly overwhelming, but Billy didn't move for a full minute, wanting to be sure it was dead. He could see where the first two rounds had hit—the shotgun pulled slightly to the left, though the final shot had been dead on—chipping away at the thick armor that shaded its beady black eyes.

What is *it?* He stared down at the horror, not sure he wanted to know. It had to be connected to the dogs and walking dead, to the T-virus. That journal he'd found *had* said something about even small doses causing changes in size and aggressiveness . . .

Which means this guy must have snorted a couple of gallons, minimum. Accidentally? No chance. The journal also said something about a laboratory. And controlling the effects of the virus, about how until they could control it, the company was "playing with fire."

The implications were clear enough. Maybe the T-virus had gotten out by accident, but this company, whatever it was, had obviously known what it could do beforehand. Had experimented with it.

For the moment, though, all that mattered was that it was dead—and he was done searching for any keycard. Screw going it alone. If the scorpion king had any brothers or sisters wandering around, Billy wanted someone else to take up the slack.

He picked up the shells he'd dropped and re-loaded. Then he carefully stepped around the massive, stinking carcass, and set off to find Rebecca. Maybe she'd had better luck than he had.

Just after she stepped into the front car, Rebecca thought she heard weapon fire, from back the way she came. She stood in the doorway, holding on to the frame, staring blankly at the one dead dog visible from her position as she strained to hear. Thunder rumbled outside. After a moment, she gave up, and walked toward the front of the train.

She moved slowly, steeling herself to see Edward again, wishing she'd thought to grab a blanket or something from the mess back in the passenger cars. Maybe a coat off one of the dead men; she certainly hadn't gotten anything else, except a rising sense of indignation with whoever had loosed the T-virus, and a headache from holding her breath. No keys, nothing to help. That train worker's body at the front of the car, where she'd met Billy, though—perhaps the key in its dead hand would turn out to be useful somehow.

She reached the turn in the corridor and forced herself past it, skirting the pool of fluids that had leaked from the dog—

—and Edward was gone.

Rebecca stopped, stared. The second dog was still there—but a wad of red gauze and a few bloody splatters were all that remained where Edward's body had been. That, and the thick smell of rot. Cool, wet air breezed in through the windows, but the smell was too strong for it.

Everything seemed to move in slow motion as she looked down, saw the tracks in the dog blood. She followed them with her gaze, looked toward the front, seeing the boot prints in red, smeared, as though whoever had worn them was drunk, or . . . or sick . . .

No. She'd felt for a pulse.

Time slowed even more, her gaze finally rising from the floor. She saw the edge of a bare arm, someone standing just out of sight at the end of the hall. Someone tall. Someone wearing boots.

"No," she said, and Edward stepped away from the wall, stepped into view. When he saw her, his bloodless lips opened, a moan emerging. He staggered toward her, his face gray, his eyes filmed almost white.

"Edward?"

He kept walking, reeling really, his blood-drenched shoulder trailing along the wall, his arms slack at his sides, his face empty and mindless. This was Edward, this was her buddy, and she raised her handgun, taking a step back, taking aim.

"Don't make me," she said, a part of her mind wondering at how deathlike the virus made its victims seem, *must have slowed his heart rate—*

Edward moaned again. He sounded desperately hungry, and though his eyes were barely visible through the haze of white, she could see them well enough to understand that this wasn't Edward anymore. He staggered closer.

"Be at peace," she whispered, and shot him, the round drilling a neat hole in his left temple. He stood perfectly still for a beat, his expression of dull hunger unchanging, and then collapsed to the floor.

Rebecca was still standing there, aiming at the corpse of her friend when Billy found her a few minutes later.

FIVE

William Birkin hurried through the underbelly of the water treatment plant, spooked by the echoing *clang* of his footsteps through the cavernous corridors as he made his way toward control B on the first basement level. The place felt cold and dead, like a tomb—which was not a bad analogy at all, except he knew what wandered behind the locked doors he passed, knew that he was surrounded by an abundance of life, such as it was. Somehow, that awareness made the distant echoes of his every movement seem that much more sacrilegious, like shouting in a mortuary.

Which it is, really. They're not dead yet. Your colleagues, your friends . . .

Get a grip on yourself. They all knew this was a possibility, all of them. Bad luck, is all.

Bad luck for them. He and Annette had been at the facility downtown when the spill had occurred, finalizing the breakdown of the new synthesis.

He'd reached the executive stairwell at the back of B4 and started to climb, wondering if Wesker was already waiting. Probably. Birkin was running late, he hadn't wanted to leave his work for even a moment, and Albert Wesker was a precise and punctual man, among other things. A soldier. A researcher. A sociopath.

And maybe he was the one. Maybe he leaked it. It was possible; Wesker's loyalties lay with Wesker, always had, and though he'd been with Umbrella for a long time, Birkin knew he was looking for an exit. On the other hand, crapping in his own backyard wasn't his style, and Birkin had known the man for twenty years, give or take. If Wesker *had* caused the leak, he certainly wouldn't be sticking around to see what happened next.

Birkin topped the flight, made a turn and started up the next. Allegedly, the elevators still worked, but he didn't want to risk it. There was no one around to help if something went wrong. No one but Wesker, and for all he knew, the S.T.A.R.S. commander had decided to go home.

At the top of the second flight, Birkin heard

something, a soft sound from behind the door that marked the second basement level. He paused a moment, imagining some poor soul pressed against the door on the other side, perhaps mindlessly beating his or her dying body against the obstacle again and again, vaguely wishing to be free. When the infection had originally been identified, the internal doors had locked automatically, trapping most of the infected workers and escaped test subjects. The main pathways were clear, at least to and from the control rooms.

He glanced at his watch, and started up the final flight. He didn't want to miss Wesker if he was still around.

So, if Wesker didn't do it, then who? How? They'd all thought it was an accident; he still had until a few hours ago, when Wesker had called him about the train. That was one accident too many. Lord knew there were enough people who had reason to sabotage Umbrella, but it wasn't easy to obtain even a low-level clearance pass for any of the Raccoon labs.

What if . . . Wesker had said something about the company wanting real data on the virus, not just sims but hands-on; maybe they had unleashed it themselves, sent in one of their squads to pop a cork that shouldn't have been popped, so to speak.

Or maybe this is how they plan to get to the G

virus. Create all this chaos, then slip in and steal it.

Birkin's jaw tightened. No. They didn't know yet how close he was, and wouldn't know until he was goddamn good and ready. He'd taken precautions, hidden things, and Annette had bribed the watchdogs to keep away. He'd seen it happen too many times, the company taking away a doctor's research because they wanted instant results, handing it over to new blood . . . and in at least two cases that he knew of personally, the original scientist had been eliminated, the better to keep him from moving to the competition.

Not me. And not the G virus. It was his life's work, but he'd destroy it before he'd let it be taken away.

He reached the control room he wanted, an observation platform, really, that shared space with the plant's backup generator, now thankfully silent. The lights were down, but as he walked around the mesh catwalk, he could see Wesker sitting in front of the observation screens, his back outlined by the glow from the monitors. As he often did, Wesker wore his sunglasses, an affectation that had always unnerved Birkin; the guy could see in the dark.

Before he'd announced his presence, Wesker was beckoning him over, raising a hand without even looking over his shoulder.

"Come look at this."

His voice was commanding, urgent. Birkin hurried to join him, leaning over the console to see what had Wesker so interested.

His attention was fixed on a scene from the training facility, what looked like the video library on the second floor. A trainee was wandering the room, obviously infected, his fatigues stained with blood and other fluids; he looked positively wet, but Birkin didn't notice anything particularly unusual about him otherwise.

"I don't see—" he began, but Wesker cut him off. "Wait."

Birkin watched as the young man—a young man who wouldn't be getting much older, thanks to the T-virus—ran into a small desk at the side of the room, then turned and started back toward the computer banks, lurching as all the carriers did, the camera following the movement. Just as he was about to ask Wesker what he was looking for, he saw it.

"There," Wesker said.

Birkin blinked, not sure what he'd seen. As he'd turned again at the computer banks, the trainee's right arm had elongated, thinned, stretched almost all the way to the floor, then snapped back into place. It had taken barely a second.

"That's the third time in the last half hour or so," Wesker said softly.

The trainee continued to roam the small room,

once again indistinguishable from any of the other doomed people pictured on the tiny screens.

"An experiment we didn't know about?" Birkin asked, though it was unlikely. They were both as deep inside as anyone outside of HQ.

"No."

"Mutation?"

"You're the scientist, you tell me," Wesker said.

Birkin gave it a second's thought, then shook his head. "I suppose it's possible, but . . . No, I don't think so."

They watched the soldier in silence for another moment, but he only crossed the room again; nothing stretched or changed. Birkin didn't know what they had seen, exactly, but he didn't like it, not at all. In the complicated series of equations that his life had become, between his work and family, between the disasters in Raccoon and his dreams of engineering the perfect virus, this was an unknown. This was something new.

A crackle of static burst into the quiet, an unknown man's voice emerging from the hiss. "ETA ten minutes, over."

That had to be Umbrella's cleanup crew, for the train. Wesker had said they were on their way when he'd called. Wesker tapped a button. "Affirmative. Radio when objective is reached. Over and out."

He tapped the button again, and the two men

went back to watching the unknown soldier, each lost in thoughts all their own. He didn't know about Wesker, but he was starting to think that it might be time to get out of Raccoon.

"Rebecca."

She didn't answer or turn around, only lowered her weapon. Billy wished there was something he could say, but figured he was better off keeping his mouth shut. The scenario was clear enough; the man on the floor was in a S.T.A.R.S. uniform, probably a friend, and he'd been infected.

He gave her a moment, but didn't think they could afford more than one. He couldn't be sure, but the train seemed to be picking up speed. If it was a runaway, they would crash and likely die. If someone was controlling it, they needed to know who and why.

"Rebecca," he said again, and this time she turned, unashamed of the tears she wiped away. She blinked up at him.

"Did I hear you firing a few minutes ago?" she asked.

Billy nodded, tried a smile but it didn't come off. "Monster bug. You?"

"Dog," she said, and wiped away a last tear. "And . . . and someone I used to know."

He shifted uncomfortably, both of them silent for

a beat. Then she sighed, pushed her bangs off her forehead. "Tell me you found the keys," she said.

"Something like that," he said, hefting the shotgun.

"Won't work," she said, and sighed again. "It has magnetic bolts, like a bank vault or something."

"On a passenger train?" Billy asked.

Rebecca shrugged. "It's privately owned. Umbrella."

The pharmaceutical company. Between the court-martial and sentencing, Billy hadn't given much thought to where he was headed for execution, but now he remembered—Raccoon City, the closest thing this area had to a metropolis, was where the megacorporation had originally set up shop.

"They have their own train?"

She nodded. "Umbrella's all over around here. Offices, medical research, laboratories . . ."

"We heard today about the Arklay lab . . . and we're being sent in to check it out next week." Raccoon forest, Raccoon City itself, was nestled in the Arklay mountains.

Rebecca's thoughts seemed to be turning in the same direction. "You don't think—"

"I don't know," Billy said. "And right now, it doesn't matter, anyway. We still have to get through that door."

She started to turn back toward the front of the train, then seemed to think better of it, perhaps not wanting to see her friend. She looked at the floor, spoke in a low voice.

"There's a body up by the door, a man holding a key," she said. "Maybe it opens something useful."

"Wait here a sec," Billy said. He stepped past her and moved forward, stopping at the corridor's end. The decrepit corpse of a train worker was huddled by the locked door, the body she'd been bent over at their first meeting. Sure enough, he had a metal key in one stiff hand. Billy pried it free, held it up in the low light. The small tag attached to it read, DINING CAR.

That's wonderfully helpful, thank you so much. He set it aside, then spent a minute going through the man's coat, coming up with a pack of cards and a handful of lint-covered breath mints in one front pocket . . . And in the other, a few more keys on a small ring. Two were unlabeled, but a third had CON-DUCTOR's etched into the metal. Billy pocketed them, and after a moment's thought, he knelt and carefully removed the man's coat, grimacing at the cold, spongy feel of his flesh. The poor guy didn't appear to have caught the virus, but person or persons un-known had worked him over with their teeth; he was a mess, his face and hands missing large, ragged chunks of skin and muscle.

Billy walked back to where Rebecca stood, paus-ing to cover the dead S.T.A.R.S. team member with the coat. It only concealed his face and upper body, but he figured anything was an improvement, for the girl's sake. She nodded gratefully at him as he approached, but said nothing.

"The key you saw was for the dining car, which we've already sampled," he said. He pulled the ringed set out of his pocket. "But these might open something."

They were standing near the door labeled as the conductor's office. Billy held up the marked key. With a nod from Rebecca, he slid the key into the lock; it turned easily. He readied his weapon and pushed the door open, ready to fire at anything that didn't identify itself in their first second of contact.

There was no one. Billy relaxed slightly, stepping into the office. Rebecca waited in the doorway, her weapon also drawn, looking down at a small desk littered with papers. She rustled through them as Billy threw the rest of the tiny cabin.

"Schedules, letters . . . Here's something called a 'Hookshot Operator Manual,'" Rebecca said. "Memos from maintenance, a note about a ring lock, whatever that is, kitchen order forms . . ."

Billy opened the closet while she continued to rattle off the desk's clutter. A couple of signs, postcards and notes tacked to the inside of the door, ledgers, a locked briefcase. Billy picked up the briefcase, shook it. Something inside rattled, but it was very light; something like a keycard, perhaps? Not likely, but he could always hope.

He examined the lock, frowning. There was no keyhole, though there was an indentation on the front, in the shape of a circle. He jiggled the handle. It was solidly locked. He could probably take the thing apart, but it was well made, it would take time they couldn't spare . . .

"A minute ago, you said something about a ring lock?" He asked.

Rebecca pushed a few papers aside. "Ah . . . Here. It's just a handwritten note, says, 'Means of access in case, scattered ring lock, two parts.'"

In case of what? He started to shrug, then felt a flush of excitement. In *case*. The card *was* in the case, he could feel it. He looked closer at the lock, suddenly remembering the unusual silver ring he'd found upstairs, before his run-in with the scorpion-thing. The indentation on the lock was notched like the ring had been.

But the note says two parts, and—

"Hey, I found a ring, at the back of the train," Rebecca said. Billy looked up as Rebecca pulled a gold ring from her index finger, knowing even before she handed it over that it was the second part.

"I think we have a winner," Billy said, actually smiling, a real smile for the first time since . . . since he didn't know when. There would be a radio in the engineer's compartment, and controls, and maybe a map for how the hell to get out of the woods.

They were almost out of this, he was sure of it. He had no idea.

Someone had actually started the goddamn train. There was a chance that one of the workers was still alive, but Wesker figured it more likely that one of the mush-brain carriers had fallen into the controls. In any event, the 'copters's pilot hadn't even hesitated, had only changed the ETA by a few moments. The timing was lucky; unstopped, the train would head straight for the training facility, would crash if it was unmanned, and the last thing they needed was to draw attention to any of the infected lockdown areas.

"We're deploying now, over."

Wesker waited. He could hear the sound of the helicopter in the background, could even hear the men's drop lines whipping in the wind. He half wished he was there, about to step onto the doomed train as it sped through the storming night, his weapon drawn, the walking diseased waiting to be laid to rest in a blast of blood and bone . . .

Birkin interrupted the pleasant fantasy, his voice and manner anxious as he reached out to cover the microphone with one pale hand. "We're sure this is the virus, right? I mean, we're not dealing with a hijacking, or . . . or a mechanical error, perhaps? I mean, do we know for certain that this team is here to handle the train?"

Wesker sighed internally. William Birkin was an intelligent man, but also obsessively paranoid. His conviction that Umbrella wanted to steal his work was almost childlike in its intensity.

"We're sure," he answered. "What else could it be, if not the virus?"

Birkin nodded toward the monitor where they'd seen the soldier with the rubbery arm. "Maybe something to do with that."

Wesker shrugged. It was a mutation, it had to be. Unusual, but hardly impossible. "I doubt it. Don't worry, William. No one at the top knows about your precious G virus." Not exactly true, but Wesker wasn't in a hand-holding mood. "As for the train . . . perhaps the T is simply better at adapting than we thought."

Birkin wasn't buying, which wasn't a surprise; Wesker didn't, either. If the infection of the train was an accident, he was his Aunt Maddie's teapot, as it were.

"The mansion, the labs, the train . . . Who did it?" Birkin asked softly. "And why?"

One of the cleanup pair broke in. "We're down, over." The background *whup-whup* sound of the helicopter's blades had been replaced by the rhythmic rumble of a moving train.

About goddamn time. "Excellent," Wesker said, again covering the microphone so that he could answer Birkin.

"That's irrelevant. What matters now is that this doesn't get out, that it doesn't go any further. The train has to be destroyed. All of the evidence has to go, William, surely you can see that. There's no problem here. Don't create one."

He uncovered the mike. "How far are you from the nearest branch line, over?"

"No more than ten minutes, probably—"

Wesker waited through a blur of static. "Yes? Didn't copy that, over?"

There was a shrill burst of feedback, loud enough to hurt. Wesker recoiled, saw Birkin wincing at the noise—

—and then there was screaming, both of the men on the train screaming in unison.

"Ah, God, what the—"

"Jesus!"

"Get 'em off me! Get 'em off!"

"No! Nooo! Noo—"

There were several muffled bursts of automatic gunfire, a man's wordless cry of pain and terror surpassing the sound—and then there was nothing but static.

Wesker ground his teeth together as behind him, Birkin started to babble in panic. It seemed that there was a problem after all.

* * *

They stood in front of the locked door, Rebecca holding the keycard and feeling a triumph that was all out of proportion to what they'd actually done. She figured she was probably emotionally worn out; it was no big deal, they'd found a couple of rings, opened a briefcase. Regardless, she felt like they'd solved the riddle of the goddamn Sphinx.

Billy motioned for her to open the door, his head cocked to one side. He was still listening. He'd sworn he'd heard a helicopter outside when they'd gone to retrieve the ring, and someone shouting a moment later. Rebecca hadn't heard anything. He was probably as wrung out as she was, considering—

—*considering he was on his way to be executed. Don't start making comparisons, here. Whatever he's done to help you out, he's an animal. Forgetting it could cost you your life.*

Right. As soon as she made it to a working radio, their little truce was over. She swiped the card through the reader, and the small red light changed to green. The door clicked, and Billy pushed it open.

The sound of the train became a roar, the door opening into a grated walkway that was partially exposed to the elements. Wind and mist sprayed over them as Billy and then Rebecca stepped outside. To the right was a locked cage of equipment that ran the length of the car; to the left, only a guard rail and the violent night whipping past. Ahead, another car, what had to be the driver's compartment; it was hard to tell in the dark. Rebecca grabbed the railing when she realized just how fast the train was going; the thing was really rocking along the tracks, and—

Oh.

Rebecca hesitated as Billy hurried a few steps ahead, then crouched down in front of a fallen man or woman. There was a second form a meter or so past the first; both were dressed in riot gear, their faces hidden behind shaded glass.

S.W.A.T.? When did they get here? And why only two? As she moved closer, she could see that they were both shining with slime, the same thick goo that those leeches in the dining car had excreted . . . And their gear, all Kevlar and steel-weave, was unmarked. They weren't RCPD, or military.

Billy was looking at the mesh wall to their right. Rebecca followed his gaze, saw what looked like a giant web of dark strings fixed to the inside of the gate, hanging with about a thousand semi-translucent sacs.

Egg sacs. For the leeches.

Rebecca shuddered, and then Billy was standing again, shaking his head. He had to shout to be heard over the thundering train.

"It's no good! They're dead!"

99

Rebecca had figured as much, but she wasn't going to take his word for it. She pushed past him and checked both bodies for signs of life, noticing the strange, puckered hemorrhaging on their exposed and pallid skin. Billy was right . . . and maybe he'd been right about hearing a scream, too. In spite of the rain, both of the bodies were still warm.

She stood up and grabbed the railing again, following Billy to the next car. She just had time to wonder what the hell they were going to do if they ran across another lock, and then Billy was pushing the door open.

They stepped out of the rain and into a relatively small driver's compartment, clean and orderly except for the thin, even layer of slime covering the control console at the front. Rebecca's ears rang in the sudden near-silence as the door closed behind her, but she was more concerned with the number of blinking red lights that lit up the glistening console.

Billy stepped up and studied the myriad control panels for a moment, then tapped at a keyboard set in front of a small screen. The screen remained blank. He looked back at her with a bleak expression.

"The controls are locked," he said.

Rebecca fished the keycard out of her vest pocket. There were no numbers on either side, nothing they could input. She moved to his side, trying to ignore the rain lashing the windshield, the dizzying blur of the woods, and punched a few buttons. The keys *felt* locked, they didn't depress completely. She started looking for anything with the word EMERGENCY on it.

"Here," Billy said, reaching for a lever that stuck out from his side of the board. When he pushed it, words started scrolling across the computer screen.

EMERGENCY BRAKES—FRONT AND REAR TERMINALS MUST BE ACTIVATED BEFORE APPLYING BRAKES. RESTORE POWER TO REAR TERMINAL?

The controls she'd seen at the back of the train. Billy quickly typed in YES.

POWER TO REAR BRAKE TERMINAL RESTORED.

"Thank God," Rebecca said. "Do it, stop this thing." The train seemed to be going impossibly faster, the rumble of the engines louder than before, rising to fever pitch.

Billy pushed the lever. It moved easily, too easily, and more words scrolled across the screen.

REAR BRAKE SEQUENCE MUST BE ACTIVATED BEFORE EMERGENCY BRAKES ARE APPLIED.

"Oh, you gotta be shitting me," Billy said, his lips curled. "We can't put on the emergency brakes from the goddamn *control room?*"

"We probably can, just not without authorization," Rebecca said. "Manually, though . . . I saw the rear terminal; it's on the back of the last car. I'll go."

Billy shook his head, looking out at the passing darkness, passing too quickly. "No, let me. No offense, but I think I can run faster. Is there an intercom system? I can signal you when it's on."

They both started to look, but the console was crowded with unmarked switches and panels; it'd take too long to figure out. Rebecca started to tell him he'd just have to run—and from how much faster the train seemed to be going now, he should probably sprint—when she remembered Edward.

"Edward's radio," she said. "He had it before he—it should still be on him."

Billy was already turning toward the door. "I'll get it on the way."

"Be careful," she said.

He nodded, casting another look out the window. "Just be ready to hit the brakes up here. I have the feeling we're going to stop pretty soon anyway, one way or another."

He opened the door to a blast of noise, then was gone.

The seconds ticked by. Rebecca made sure her radio was receiving, then kept her hand on the brake lever, staring out at the onrushing night. The train took a curve too fast and she closed her eyes for a beat, willing the out-of-control engine to stay on the track, imagining that she could actually feel the wheels rise up and then fall back into place. Billy was right; one way or another, they weren't going to be going much farther.

What's taking so long? It had only been a few minutes, but that was long enough. She grabbed the radio, pressed TRANSMIT.

"Billy, come in. What's your status, over."

Nothing.

"Billy?" She waited, counted slowly to five, her heart starting to trip over itself. She could see another curve coming up ahead. "Billy, come in!"

Shit! Maybe he hadn't found the radio, or had forgotten to turn it on. Or there was something wrong with the controls, he couldn't activate the terminal.

Or maybe he's dead. Maybe something got to him.

The train railed around the curve, and this time there was no imagining; the train tipped too heavily, racing ever faster as it rattled back down, and another curve like that one, it was all over. She'd have to go back herself, there was no time but there was no other option, either—

"Rebecca, now!"

Rebecca saw a blur to the right of the train, there and gone so quickly that she didn't know what it was until it was past—a station platform. *The* station platform, and that meant the only thing left ahead was wherever they stored the goddamn thing, and that meant it might already be too late.

S.D. PERRY

"Hang on!" she shouted at the radio, grabbing the brake lever, twisting it as hard as she could—and something was rushing at the front window, a darkness deeper than the night, a tunnel. The brakes were squealing, *screaming* as the train roared into the black, broke through some flimsy barrier, wood flying across the windshield, the train tipping again, this time not tipping back.

Rebecca heard her own scream join the train's as they hit the ground and started to slide, metal rending, sparks flaring up like hellish fireworks. The wall became the floor, Rebecca slamming into it as the engine slammed into something even harder and all the lights went out.

Six

Billy woke up to pain and the smell of burning synthetics. He opened his eyes, blinking, assessing his surroundings as quickly as his muddled mind could manage, which wasn't very quickly at all. He was on his back, looking up at a high, blank ceiling. Firelight flickered all around him, shadows of rubble and rock dancing across part of a wall to his left. Somehow, he was inside.

The brakes, the train . . . Rebecca?

That woke him up. He pushed himself to a sitting position, was surprised and relieved to realize he had a strained shoulder and a few scrapes, but nothing worse.

"Rebecca?" he called, and coughed. Wherever he

was, the billowing smoke from the wreck was starting to build up. He, they, had to move.

He stood, cradling his right arm as he looked
around. The train had crashed into a warehouse, it
looked like—a giant, empty space, concrete, a scaf-
folding off to one side, a few hooded lights overhead. It wasn't very well lit, but when he looked
down, he saw a dented train track beneath his feet,
and realized they had probably crashed into the
train's maintenance terminal. Wherever that was.

"Rebecca?" He called again, surveying the
wreckage. There were numerous piles of blasted
concrete and puddles of burning oil all around. The
engine was on its side, the other cars piled up behind
it, blocking what had to be a monster hole in the
wall. He had no idea where to look for the young
S.T.A.R.S. member. As soon as he'd activated the
rear brakes he had started running back toward the
front; he must have been thrown from the back passenger car . . .

"Uunh." A slumped shadow stirred near a pile of
smoking rock.

"Rebecca!" He stumbled forward, hoping she
was all right. She had sounded panicked when she'd
called, when he hadn't answered, but he'd been too
busy punching buttons to talk. Now he was sorry;
she was just a kid, after all, and had been scared shit-
less. *I should have reassured her, something—*

He reached the crumpled, battered body, and started to kneel beside her. She was face down, her clothes shredded.

"Billy?"

Billy turned, saw Rebecca walking toward him, her nine-millimeter in hand. She had a trickle of blood seeping from her hairline, but appeared to be in good shape otherwise—

—and the person in front of him rolled over, moaning again, reaching one bloody hand up to grasp at his face. Rotting fingers trailed across his cheek.

"Gah!" With a wordless cry of disgust he reeled back, fell on the floor. He couldn't tell if the slow-moving creature was male or female, so much of its face and body had been damaged, either by the disease or from the crash. It crawled to its knees, turning its disfigured face toward Billy. Its mouth hung open, and blood-tinted drool poured from between its broken teeth as it reached for him again.

"Get clear," Rebecca said, and he was only too glad to comply, scrambling backward on his hands, the loose handcuff digging painfully into the flesh of his left palm, pushing with his feet. She aimed and fired twice, both rounds finding the once-human's already fractured skull, ending what was left of its life. It settled to the concrete with a sound almost like a sigh.

Billy stood up, and they both spent a few tense seconds scanning the wreckage for any other bodies. If there were more, they were hidden.

"Thanks," he said, looking back at the pathetic creature. She'd spared it further suffering, at least—and with two clean head shots. He was surprised and not a little impressed at her level of skill. "Are you okay?"

"Yeah. I've got a killer headache, but that's all. My second crash of the day, too."

"Really?" Billy asked. "What was the first?"

She smiled, started to speak—then abruptly stopped, her expression turning cool, and Billy felt a pang of real unhappiness; she'd obviously remembered who she was talking to. In spite of everything, she still thought he was a mass murderer.

"It's not important," she said. "Come on. We should get out of here before the smoke gets any worse."

They both still had their radios, and spent a moment looking for his gun, finding it half hidden by a crushed concrete block not far from where he'd woken up. The shotgun was history. Neither of them suggested searching the train for it; the small fires were dying out, but the thick layer of black smoke that hovered at the ceiling was growing by the minute.

They moved around the vast room, finding only a

single door some twenty meters from the wrecked engine and very little else. Billy hoped it led to fresh air, to freedom for himself and safety for the girl. Standing at the door, he looked back at the smoldering crash, felt one corner of his mouth curve up.

"Well, at least we managed to stop the train," he said.

Rebecca nodded, her smile weak but game. "We managed," she replied.

They turned back to the door. Taking a deep breath, Billy reached out and turned the handle, pushing it open.

It was surreal, watching the train crash into the basement of the training facility on a screen, hearing the dull thunder of the crash a beat later. They felt it, too, a very faint rumble in the walls all around them. In seconds, the camera lens was obscured by smoke.

"We should get out of here, now," Birkin said, pacing behind Wesker's chair. He wasn't worried about fire, the old terminal was practically made out of cement—but a train crash was hard to miss, and not every cop and fireman in the vicinity was on Umbrella's payroll. The facility was isolated, but it would only take a phone call from one concerned citizen and Umbrella's bioweapons work would be exposed.

Wesker didn't even seem to be listening. He

tapped at the monitor controls, shifting camera per-
spectives through other parts of the facility, searching for something. He'd barely said a word since the
final transmission from the cleanup crew.

"Are you listening to me?" Birkin asked, not for
the first time in the past few minutes. He was tense,
and Wesker's cavalier attitude wasn't helping.

"I hear you, William," Wesker said, still watching
the screens. "If you want to leave, leave."

"Well? Aren't you coming?"

"Oh, in a while," he answered, his tone calm and
even. "I just want to check on a few things."

"Like what? I'd say the train is pretty much
cleaned up. That's why we came, isn't it?"

Wesker didn't answer, only kept watching the
screens. Birkin's hands clenched into fists. God, the
man could be insufferable! That was the problem
with sociopaths. The inability to empathize tended to
make them completely self-centered.

I've *got work to do,* Birkin thought, looking toward
the door. Work, a family . . . he wasn't going to wait
around for Joe Firefighter to come knocking, looking
for an explanation as to why there were zombies wandering around the crash site . . .

"Ah, there we are," Wesker said, thumbing a key
beneath one of the screens. It was the main lobby of
the facility, built to welcome execs and grunts alike
into the less-than-legal world of White Umbrella.

And as they watched, a hand came up through the floor, pushing aside a square cover.

That's the old access tunnel, leads from the terminal. Birkin leaned forward, curious in spite of himself.

A man with an elaborate tattoo on one arm crawled out of the dark square in the northwest corner of the room, followed by a small woman in a S.T.A.R.S. uniform, a girl, really. Both carried handguns, and looked around the finely decorated lobby with expressions Birkin couldn't read from the small screen.

"Who on earth are those people?" he asked.

"The girl is a S.T.A.R.S. rookie, B team," Wesker said. "No one of consequence. The male I don't recognize."

"Do you think—were they on the train?"

"Had to have been," Wesker said.

Birkin felt a new surge of panic. "What are we going to do?"

Wesker glanced up at him, one eyebrow arched. "What do you mean?"

"They—she's with S.T.A.R.S., and who knows who he's working for. What if they escape?"

"Don't be obtuse, William. They won't escape. Even if the facility wasn't locked down, the place is overrun with carriers. All they have to do is open a door or two, and they'll cease to be of any concern."

Wesker's bland tone was chilling, but he had a point. The chances of anyone getting out of the facility were slim to none.

As they watched, the two intruders moved carefully around the big room, one of the only rooms in the building free of the infected, both sweeping their weapons side to side. After a thorough check, the girl walked up the grand staircase, stopping at the small landing mid-floor. There was a large portrait there of Dr. Marcus—and the girl seemed surprised by it, as though she recognized him. The tattooed man joined her, and Birkin could see him reading aloud from the small plaque beneath the portrait— DOCTOR JAMES MARCUS, FIRST GENERAL MANAGER.

Birkin shifted uncomfortably. He hated that picture. It reminded him of how he'd gotten his real start in Umbrella, not something he liked to think about—

"Attention. This is Doctor Marcus."

Birkin jumped, looking around with wide eyes, his heart pounding. Wesker didn't flinch, but turned up the sound on the console's ancient intercom as the voice of a man ten years dead rang through the empty spaces and corridors of the entire complex.

"Please be silent as we reflect upon our company motto. Obedience breeds discipline. Discipline breeds unity. Unity breeds power. Power is life."

The man and woman on the screen were looking

around as well, but Birkin barely glanced in their direction. He grabbed Wesker's shoulder, unnerved. It was a recording, one he hadn't heard since he and Wesker had still been students at the facility. *Where?—who?—*

Wesker brushed his hand away, nodding toward the screen, where the picture was fading. It seemed to blink—and then they were looking at a young man in another location. Birkin didn't recognize the room, but the young man staring back at them seemed almost familiar. He had long hair and dark eyes, was probably in his early twenties—and he had a sharp, cruel smile, as thin and cutting as a steel blade.

"Who are you?" Wesker asked, surely not expecting an answer, there was no audio set up—

The young man laughed, the sound pouring out of the intercom like dark silk. It wasn't possible—he didn't wear a headset, wasn't near any part of the com system—but they could hear him clearly nonetheless.

"It was I who scattered the T-virus in the mansion," he said, his voice cold. His smile sharpened. "Needless to say, I contaminated the train, too."

"What?" Birkin blurted. "Why?"

The young man's cold voice seemed to deepen. "Revenge. On Umbrella."

He turned away from the camera, raising his arms

to the shadows. Birkin and Wesker both leaned in, trying to see what he was doing, but they could only see movement in the darkness, hear something like water—

The young man turned back to look at them, his smile ever sharper—and from out of the shadows behind him stepped a tall, distinguished man in a suit and tie, his white hair slicked back, his features lined with age but powerful, commanding. It was the same face that graced the portrait in the lobby.

"Dr. Marcus?" Birkin gasped.

"Ten years ago, Dr. Marcus was murdered by Umbrella," the young man said, his voice almost a snarl. "And *you* helped them. Didn't you?"

He laughed again, that dark and silken laugh, a laugh that promised no mercy as Birkin and Wesker stared, stunned into silence by the visible, living presence of a man they'd watched die a decade earlier.

The young man sang, and the many, his children, turned the camera away, manipulated the controls that allowed his voice to travel. He'd said all he intended, at least for the moment; there was much to do, many choices to consider. Things were unfolding, always unfolding in new directions.

He sang a slower song and the image and body of Marcus collapsed, reverted to the children. They gathered at his feet, coursed up and over his body, stroking him, adoring him. Waiting for him to decide what was next.

There was no plan, beyond Umbrella's destruction. He had and would continue to employ whatever means came to hand—the virus, the many, the false images that the many were capable of creating, like Marcus; he had been for Albert and William's benefit, had undoubtedly left them afraid and confused.

The young man smiled. How fortuitous, that they of all people should be witness to the downfall. With luck, he would have the opportunity to see them expire, to stand by as they had once stood by, pitilessly watching their mentor in his last struggling moments . . . Though their deaths were meaningless in the grander picture. What mattered was that Umbrella would soon be no more.

He considered the man and woman from the train, how he might use them now that they'd entered the complex. His first inclination had been to kill them, to keep them from interfering, but that seemed a waste; after all, wasn't Umbrella now their enemy, too? They would fight for their lives, fight to be free—and if they succeeded, they would draw immediate attention to the disaster, what he had always seen as the cross atop Umbrella's grave. Destroying their laboratories, killing their employees—they could always build new labs, hire new people. Once the spotlight of the international press turned toward Umbrella, however, their ruin would be complete . . . And the world would finally know his name.

The facility had been locked down, of course. It had been designed with almost as many door puzzles and concealed passages as Trevor's mansion, built a decade earlier. Oswell Spencer, one of Umbrella's co-founders, had been obsessed with spy movies and books, and as paranoid as any megalomaniac, which made for an extremely secure lockdown. There were hidden keys, doors that wouldn't open without missing pieces, even a room or two designed to trap unwary intruders. It wouldn't be easy for anyone to escape.

But there were other false men seeded throughout the complex, men created by the many, each prepared to infect any and all who came near; they had helped spread the virus in the first place. He could use them now to open the training facility, to collect keys and unlock doors, to ensure that the man and woman would at least have a chance to survive. It was a slight chance—the false men weren't the only virus carriers roaming the halls—but they had already proven themselves to be more resilient than most.

The young man laughed, thinking of Albert and William, wondering what they were thinking; James Marcus's brightest students, working damage control for Umbrella. After all these years. It was an irony beyond measure.

The children cooed, covered him, delighted in his laughter and sang their own sweet song, a song of chaos and interdependence as their cool, slick bodies, filled with the blood of his enemies, merged and enveloped him.

". . . breeds power. Power is life."

The powerful voice faded, the great hall falling silent once more. It had to be a recording or something, it didn't sound live, but someone had turned it on—and she thought she had an idea of who. She turned her attention back to the portrait of Dr. Marcus and felt a shiver run down her spine.

"Well, *that* was creepy," Billy said.

"Not as creepy as seeing him on the train," Rebecca said, nodding at the portrait. "Made out of slime bugs."

"Maybe it's another stage of the disease or something," Billy said.

Rebecca nodded, though she doubted it. The zombielike people they'd seen on the train and the man in the dining car—who appeared to be one James Marcus—didn't have the same symptoms.

"Or maybe the leeches infect some people, and . . . I don't know, take other people over," she said.

"Yeah," Billy said. He ran one hand through his hair and smiled at her, a surprisingly pleasant smile. "Anyway. You should probably find a phone or something, call your friends in."

His tone was dismissive. Rebecca's hand tightened on her nine-millimeter. "What are you going to do?"

Billy turned and started down the staircase, his step light. "Thought I might take a walk," he called back to her.

She followed him as he walked to the front door, not sure what to do, what to say. She seriously doubted that she could shoot him, not after he'd saved her life, but she couldn't just let him leave, either. "I don't think that's such a good idea," she said.

He pulled the door open. Cool, humid night air swept in, though the rain had turned to drizzle. "Much as I appreciate the concern, I think I've earned a head start, don't you? So let's just—"

He stopped in mid-stride, in mid-sentence, looking out at the rainswept landscape in front of them. The facility, it seemed, had been built into the side of a hill. In front of them was a paved walkway, big enough to be a road, that stretched out ten meters—and then ended abruptly, falling off into nothingness.

Together, they walked out to the edge of the path. There were light posts on either side of the front door; only one of them was working, but it was enough to see that without a rope, neither of them was going anywhere. The path ended in a jagged line of rubble, atop a steep slope that dropped down at least five meters, probably more. It was too dark to tell much of anything.

"You were saying?" Rebecca said.

"So, I'll find another door," Billy said, turning back to look at the building. It looked like an estate, was certainly decorated like some stuffy billionaire's weekend getaway, but they'd both seen the UMBRELLA TRAINING FACILITY logo stamped into the polished marble floor. Rebecca figured it was like an executive retreat or something. It had an air of abandonment, but the place had power, lights . . . Of course, all they'd seen so far was where the train had crashed, the extravagant lobby, and a half-submerged tunnel that connected the two. Not much to go on.

"I saw at least two in there, not counting whatever's at the top of the stairs," he continued. "And if all else fails, maybe I can crawl back out through the train."

"Assuming my friends don't show up first," Rebecca said. She stepped back, picked up her radio and hit the transmit signal. Billy's radio beeped in response, but that was the only response. After a long moment of radio silence, the only sound that of rain dripping off distant trees, Billy smirked.

"Assuming *you* find a phone."

God, he was irritating. She turned and started back for the house, slightly amazed, as she reached the door, that she felt safe enough to turn her back to him . . . Although if he'd wanted her dead, he'd already had ample opportunity. In spite of her intentions to the contrary, she was having trouble thinking of him as dangerous. Her instincts were telling her otherwise, and that was one of the first lessons that S.T.A.R.S. taught—you might misread your intuition, but it was never wrong.

He caught up to her as she stepped back inside— and they both stopped, staring. The painting of Marcus was gone. There was a doorway there now, a dark opening in the wall; from their angle at the bottom of the stairs, there was no way to tell what was past the opening.

She was about to tell Billy to hang back when he stepped in front of her, his weapon in hand. As he swept the area, his posture, his gaze at full alert, she was again struck by the strong feeling that he wasn't what he had originally appeared to be.

Not that I need to be protected. She moved to his side, surveying the room as she'd been trained, and together, they headed up the stairs, stopping at the landing. The new entry opened on a staircase heading down, a blank, barely lit corridor at the bottom.

"Questions, comments?" Billy asked, peering down.

"Someone wants us to go downstairs," she said.

"Kinda what I was thinking. And I'm also thinking that might not be such a good idea."

Rebecca nodded. She turned away from the opening, looking around at their options. There were two doors downstairs, one on the left wall, one on the right. On the second floor, she could see four more from where she was standing—and as she looked around, a loud *ffump* came from somewhere behind them, from somewhere down in that blank, dark hallway. It sounded like something very soft and very heavy, falling to the floor. Without speaking, they both edged away from the opening.

"So, what say we extend our truce for a little while longer?" Billy asked, and though his voice was light, he wasn't smiling.

Rebecca nodded again. "Yeah," she said, wondering what they'd gotten themselves into, and what it would take for them to get out.

SEVEN

They walked back down to the lobby floor, Billy glad that she'd agreed to keep cooperating. This place, whatever it was, was definitely bad news. She was inexperienced, but at least she wasn't nuts.

"We should split up," Rebecca said.

Billy barked a laugh, one entirely devoid of humor. "Are you nuts? Haven't you ever seen a horror movie? Besides, look what happened last time."

"We found the key to that briefcase, if I remember correctly. And what we need now is a way out of here."

"Yeah, but alive," Billy said. "This place has hostile territory written all over it. I suggested a truce in the first place because I *don't* want to die, get it?"

"You've taken care of yourself pretty good so far," she said. "I'm not saying we go get in trouble. Just open a few doors, is all. And we've got radios now."

Billy sighed. "Didn't the S.T.A.R.S. teach you about teamwork?"

"Actually, this was my first mission," Rebecca said. "Look, we take a look around, call if we find anything. I'll head upstairs, you check down here. If the radios fritz out, we meet back here in twenty minutes."

"I don't like it."

"You don't have to. Just do it."

"Sir, yes, *sir*," Billy snapped. She wasn't lacking leadership tendencies, he'd give her that—although maybe it wasn't so hard to order a convicted felon around when you worked for the law. "How old are you, anyway? I'd like to know I'm taking orders from someone more mature than your average Girl Scout."

Rebecca shot him a scowl, then turned and went back up the stairs. A few seconds later, he heard a door close.

Well. Billy looked around the lobby. *Eeny, meeny, miney . . .*

"Mo," Billy said, turning to the left wall. He'd didn't want to go it alone, he'd rather have backup, but it was probably better this way; if he found an

123

exit, he could take his walk, after all, call her to say good-bye on his way out. Leaving her behind wouldn't make him feel so hot, but she could hole up and wait for rescue; she'd be all right. He had to keep his continued health in mind; if any other S.T.A.R.S. showed up, or the RCPD, *or* the MPs, he'd be on his way back to Ragithon in a heartbeat.

He pushed the thought away as he stepped up to the door. He'd been pretty screwed up since the sentencing, filled with rage and anguish in equal parts. Since the jeep wreck he'd been able to put his date with death out of mind, a necessity if he wanted to be able to think clearly. He had to keep it up.

"Let's see what's behind door number one," he mumbled, pushing the nondescript door open—and tensed, raising the handgun, taking aim. It was a dining room, one that had once been quite elegant. Now there were two, three infected men wandering around the trashed dinner table in the center of the room, and all three were turning toward him. They all looked like zombies, their skin gray and torn, their eyes blank. One of them had a fork sticking out of one shoulder.

Billy quickly closed the door and stepped back, waiting to see if any of the creatures could manage a doorknob, the emptiness of the lobby weighing on his back like a cold stare. After a few beats he heard a shuffling against the wood and then a low, frustrated cry, the sound as mindless as the zombies seemed to be.

Well. The house, training facility, whatever it was, had been infected just like the train; that answered *that* question. He grabbed the radio, hit the transmit button.

"Rebecca, come in. We got zombies here. Over." He thought about the giant scorpion-thing and shuddered, hoping that zombies was all they had.

There was a pause, then her youthful voice crackled out. "Copy that. Do you need help? Over."

"No," Billy said, annoyed. "But don't you think we should reconsider our plans? Over?"

"This doesn't change anything," she said. "We still have to find a way out. Keep looking, and let me know what else you find. Over and out."

Great. Wondergirl was sticking to the plan. So, door number two, unless he wanted to take his chances with three of the things. He turned and walked across the room, telling himself it would be a waste of ammo, which was true. It was also true that he didn't want to shoot sick people, no matter how deranged . . . And that the zombies were seriously freaky, and if he could avoid them, he would.

He pushed the second door open, held it, his senses on high. It opened into a plush hallway that led along to his right, turning not far ahead. There was no sound, no movement, and it smelled like dust, nothing more ominous. He waited a moment, then stepped inside, letting the door settle closed behind him.

He crept down the hall, his steps muffled by thick carpet, leading around the turn with his weapon, letting out a breath when he saw that it, too, was clear. So far, so good. The hall continued on, turning again, but there was a door on the left he could try.

Billy pushed the door open—and smiled at the empty bathroom, at the row of sinks that he could see from the door.

"That reminds me," he said, stepping inside. He checked the room quickly; sinks lined two walls of the U-shaped room, four toilet stalls lining a third, discreetly out of sight from the door. As nice as the house was, it did seem to be abandoned, perhaps recently; one of the stall doors was hanging off its hinges, the toilet seat fractured, and there were a few odds and ends scattered across the floor, empty bottles, potted plants, unlikely debris for a bathroom. There was even a plastic gas tank in one of the stalls. On the other hand, there was relatively clean water in the bowl . . . Which, considering the urgency of his visit, was good enough for him.

He was just zipping up a minute later when he heard someone step into the bathroom. A single step, then a long pause . . . Then a second step.

Had he closed the door? He couldn't remember,

and silently cursed himself for the slip. He pulled his weapon and pivoted on the balls of his feet, moving silently, easing the stall door open. He couldn't see the door from where he was, but he could see part of the room reflected in a long mirror above the sinks. He kept the handgun level and waited.

A third step, and again silence. Whoever it was had wet feet, he could hear the soles of his or her shoes coming off the floor with a squelching sound—and on the fourth step, he saw a profile in the mirror, and stepped out of the stall, feeling a strange mix of horror and relief as he readied himself to fire. It was a zombie, a male, its face slick and blank, its eyes trained on nothing as it swayed slightly, balancing to stay upright. They were awful—but at least they were relatively slow. And much as he didn't like the job, killing them was surely a mercy.

The zombie took another step, moving into Billy's line of fire. Billy took careful aim, sighting just above the thing's right ear, he didn't want to waste a shot—

—and the zombie turned suddenly, quickly, faster than it had any right to move. It crouched slightly, stared at Billy through one blood-burst eye, the other looking at the wall, and reached for him, still two meters away—

—but its arm was stretching, thinning out as it

snapped toward him like a rubber band, the fabric of its wet, colorless shirt stretching with it.

Billy ducked. The thing's hand sailed over his head and slapped against the stall door with a wet *smack,* then retreated, pulled back to the inhuman body that somehow looked like a zombie.

On the train, like Marcus—

It was close enough that he could see the movement of the creature's clothes, the strange rippling effect as its arm snapped back into place. Leeches, the goddamn thing was made out of leeches, and as it took a step closer, Billy stumbled backward into the stall, firing into its wet and meaty face.

It hesitated, black ooze sliding from the wound that appeared just below its left eye—and then the wound disappeared, the faux skin gliding over it, the leeches resituating themselves. Healing themselves.

It took another step forward and Billy kicked the stall door closed, slamming it and holding it with one boot, running through ideas and discarding them just as fast.

Call for Rebecca, no time, keep shooting, not enough bullets, run, it's blocking the way—

Billy hissed in frustration—and his frenzied gaze fell on the red plastic gas can on the floor. He threw himself forward, blocking the stall door with one shoulder as he dug through his right front pocket. There, under one of the rifle shells—

He pulled out the lighter he'd taken from the train, thanking God for it, and bent down, scooped up the gas can, the loose handcuff banging against the plastic. It wasn't quite half full. *Jesus, I hope that's gas—*

The stall door was struck as though by a battering ram. Billy bounced off, then threw himself forward again, unscrewing the lid of the container with one shaking hand, his shoulder aching. The creature was strangely, horribly silent as it again charged the door, slamming into it hard enough to dent the metal.

The dizzying scent of gasoline filled the tiny stall. Billy snatched at the toilet paper roll on the wall, jerked it free—and the door smashed open, blown off its hinges by another powerful, inhuman blow. The creature stood there, swaying, its one strange eye finding Billy, targeting him.

Billy upended the can as he pushed himself to his feet, sloshing gas on himself. He thrust the can forward, pouring it onto the thing's chest.

The reaction was immediate and repulsive. The body began to writhe, to tremble, and a high-pitched squeal erupted into the room, not one voice but a thousand tiny creatures screeching as one. Thick, dark fluid began to run from seemingly every pore of its face and body.

Billy gave it a solid kick, and it staggered backward, still cohesive, still squealing, the sound piercing in the small room. He didn't know if the gas alone was enough, and wasn't going to wait and see. He flipped the lighter open and spun the wheel, holding the roll of toilet paper over the flame that sputtered to life. A second later, it was aflame.

Billy jumped out of the stall and dodged around the shrieking monster. As soon as he was past, he pivoted and threw the flaming roll of paper. It hit the leech-man just below its breastbone—and the squealing cry intensified for one horrible, deafening second as flames roared over him, enveloping him, before he collapsed into a thousand burning pieces. A black, burning puddle took shape on the tile floor, the tiny cries dying out in a matter of seconds.

A few straggling leeches crawled away from the fire, but they were disorganized, randomly sliding up the walls, slithering past his feet. Billy backed away from them, from the bubbling, dying fire, shoving the lighter back in his pocket as he neared the door.

Back in the hall, he took a deep breath, blew it out, and reached for the radio. He no longer cared what Rebecca's plans were; they were going to regroup, ASAP, and get the hell out of this place if they had to dig through the walls with their bare goddamn hands.

December 4th
When we first started, I had my doubts—but

tonight, we celebrate. We finally did it, after all this time. We're calling the new construct virus Progenitor, Ashford's idea, but I like it. We'll begin testing immediately.

March 23rd
Spencer says he's going to start a company specializing in pharmaceutical research, maybe branch into drug manufacture. As always, he's the businessman of our group. His interest in Progenitor is primarily financial, it seems, but I'm not going to complain. He wants to see us succeed, which means he'll keep us well funded; as long as he's writing checks, he can do what he likes.

August 19th
Progenitor is a marvel, but its applications are still so unsure. Just when we think we have the amplification rate documented, when we have a half dozen tests all showing the same results, everything falls apart. Ashford is still banking on working the cytokine numbers, coming at it backward, but he's dreaming. We need to keep looking.

Spencer keeps asking me to be the director of his new training facility. Maybe it's because of the business, but he's becoming intolerably pushy. In any case, I'm considering it. I need a place to properly explore new possibilities for this virus, a place where I will not be interfered with.

November 30th

Damn him. "Let's have lunch, James," he says, old comrades and fond memories. It's bullshit. He wants Progenitor ready, now. His "friends" in their White Umbrella clubhouse, with their ridiculous spy games for the rich and jaded— they want something exciting to play with, to auction off, and they don't want to wait for it. Fools. Spencer thinks that this will all come down to money, but he's wrong. That's not what any of this is about, not anymore; I don't know that it ever was. I have to strengthen my own position, guard my queen, so to speak, or I could be steamrolled.

September 19th

At last, at last! I engineered a plasmid with leech DNA and then recombined it with Progenitor— and it's stable! It was the breakthrough I've been counting on. Spencer will be happy, damn him, though I'll only let on that some progress has been made, not how much, not how. I've named *it after him, my own private joke. I'm calling it T, for Tyrant.*

October 23rd
I can't think of them as human beings. They're test subjects, that's all, that's all. I knew the research would have to come to this someday, I knew it and—and I didn't know it would be this way.

I must keep my focus. The T-virus is magnificent; they, these subjects should be honored to experience such perfection. Their lives pave a road to a higher awareness.

Test subjects. That's all. Pawns. Sometimes, pawns must be sacrificed for the greater good.

January 13th
My pets have been progressing. With their own DNA in the recombinant virus, I thought I could predict how infection would change them, but I was wrong. They've begun to colonize, like ants or bees. No individual is better than any other; they work together, a hive mind, coming together for a higher purpose. My purpose. I didn't see it at first, I was blind, but this is vastly more rewarding than the work on hu-

mans. *I must continue those tests, however—I can't let on that I've discovered the true meaning, the value of T and what it represents. Spencer would try and take it, I know he would. My king is in the open.*

February 11th
They've been watching me. I go into the lab, I see that things have been moved. They try and hide it, make everything look as it did, but I see. It's Spencer, damn his soul, he knows about my leeches, my beautiful hive, and this— this persecution won't end until one of us is dead. I can't trust anyone . . . Albert and William, perhaps, my castles, they believe in the work, but I may have to eliminate some of the others. The game draws to a close. He'll try for my queen, but the win will be mine. Check- mate, Oswell.

It was the last entry. Rebecca closed the journal and set it aside, next to the chess set that was centered on the desk. When she'd found the hidden cache, she'd thought the rudimentary maps had been the prize. There were two, one that showed what appeared to be three floors of the building's basement, including a few unmarked areas that perhaps led outside. The other seemed to be upstairs, a room labeled OBSERVA-

TORY next to a wide, open area marked BREEDING POOL. But the small, leatherbound journal, dusty and crinkled with age—she didn't know how old, exactly, but one of the entries about working with the leeches had "1988" marked in an upper corner—had been the real discovery. Written by James Marcus, presumably, apparently the creator of the T-virus, the same virus that turned men into zombies, that had infected the train and probably half of Raccoon forest, if the recent murders were any clue.

Rebecca gazed blankly at the room's strange decor, the giant chessboard that dominated the floor, her mind working. He'd obviously been crazy by the end, his ramblings about chess, about the "true meaning" of the virus. Maybe running experiments on people had driven him over the edge.

Her radio signaled. She'd no sooner pushed RECEIVE before Billy's breathless voice blared in her ear.

"Where are you? We need to regroup, now. Hello? Ah, over."

"What happened? Over."

"What happened is that I ran into another one of those leech-people in the can, and it very nearly whacked the crap out of me. Zombies we can handle, but these things—they eat bullets, Rebecca. We don't have enough ammo to hold more of them off. Over."

"They've begun to colonize, like ants or bees."

Who was controlling them? Marcus? Or had they developed their own leader, a queen?

"Okay," Rebecca said. She picked up the basement and observatory sketches she'd found, stuffed them into her vest as she stood up. After a second, she grabbed the journal, too, slipping it into a hip pocket. "Uh, meet me on the landing, where that picture of Marcus was. I may have found a way out, over."

"On my way. Watch your back, over and out."

She hurried out of the room and down the hall, moving quickly. She hadn't gotten far in her exploration, just an empty meeting room and then the office with the chess sets; thankfully, she hadn't run into anything hostile. Billy was right about the leech-men, there was no way they could handle more of those. In fact, it seemed likely that the only reason the collection of leeches on the train had stopped attacking them was because they were called off. She'd had vague hopes of staying in the nice, safe house until help arrived, but after reading Marcus's journal, hearing that the training facility was infected—they needed to get out.

After all she'd already been through tonight—the forced helicopter landing, the train, Billy, the crash, now this—she kept expecting the cavalry to ride in, for someone else to take over, to send her home to a warm dinner and bed so that she could wake up tomorrow and start her normal life again. But it seemed instead that she was being drawn even deeper into the mystery of Marcus and his creations, of Umbrella and its evil experiments.

The young man had moved to a place where the hive could comfortably gather, a large space, warm and moist and far from the possibility of daylight. The many surrounded him now, singing their tuneless song of water and darkness, but he was not soothed. He'd watched with cold fury as the girl—Rebecca, the killer had called her, and his cursed name was Billy—stole Marcus's journal, slipping it into a pocket before leaving the office. This wasn't why he'd had the desk opened for her, not at all. The map of the observatory, she was supposed to take only the map.

The two met now in front of the portrait doorway, both speaking at once, surely relating their findings, their murderous exploits. He could see the thief and the killer on a video screen at one side of his new environment—a lower level of the treatment plant—but he could see them better through the dozen pairs of rudimentary eyes watching them, the children peering out at them from the shadows. The minds of the many were powerful, able to send images to one another, to him; it was how they could work together so effectively. Rebecca and Billy had no understanding of how vulnerable they were, of how easily he could reach out and take their lives from them. They survived still only by his grace.

A thief and her murdering friend; Billy had killed a collective. He'd burned it. The few survivors were still straggling home to their master, their poor bodies scorched, showing him the death of the whole by their lack of cohesion. How had he *dared*, this unimportant man, this insect?

Rebecca held out the maps and they both studied them, too stupid, surely, to know what was expected of them. The observatory was the key to their escape, but they would undoubtedly try the basement first. It was just as well. He was no longer so sure he wanted them to go free.

They started down the stairs, disappearing from the screen, from the many's sight, but only for a second. As the couple came back into view through another camera, they stopped, staring down at the litter of arachnid bodies, dead and curled on the floor. There were four of the giant spiders, all killed mere moments before, eliminated so that Rebecca and her friend might avoid their poisonous bite. The spiders were another experiment, one doomed to fail, too slow, too difficult to handle, but lethal enough for the young man to have been concerned. He was sorry, now; watching the thief and murderer die would be his pleasure, in spite of what it did to his plans for Umbrella. The couple moved on, unaware that they were being watched by the creatures that had killed the spiders, who nested in the swollen, segmented bodies even now.

What to do? Killing them would fulfill a need in him, the need to avenge the lives of the children, the need to assert his control. But exposing Umbrella was the priority, bringing the company to ruin by laying open its stinking heart . . . which Billy and Rebecca would surely do, if they survived.

The pair followed the corridor to its end, then through the door of a long-abandoned office. After a brief consultation with their map, they continued on into a dead-end room where live specimens had once been kept. The cages were long gone, the room empty now. The young man wasn't sure why they had chosen a dead end—until he saw them move to the northeast corner, both of them looking up at the dark rectangle near the ceiling.

The ventilator shaft. It wouldn't have been labeled on the map; perhaps they believed it to be a way out. In fact, it led to—

The young man shook his head. Dr. Marcus's private chamber, the room where he'd once "entertained" certain attractive young test subjects. Why couldn't they simply leave? They'd find nothing in the private room, nothing—

—unless.

The ventilator shaft was connected to another live

specimen area, one that wasn't empty. And the creatures there hadn't been fed in days. They would very, very hungry by now. All he'd need to do would be to have the many unlatch a gate or two . . .

Rather then consider them an integral part of his plan, maybe he should think of Billy and Rebecca as test subjects. They might die—which, in truth, would probably only delay Umbrella's exposure for a short while; he was impatient, but he had to consider the entertainment value. Or, they might survive. In which case, they'd have an even greater story to tell.

The young man smiled his blade of a smile as Billy gave Rebecca a boost, lifting her up to the ventilator shaft. She crawled inside, disappearing from view. Wouldn't they be surprised, if a few of the leftovers from the primate series showed up to play?

Around him, the children cooed, the walls, the ceiling dripping with their slippery fluids. Surrounded by the many, the fate of Umbrella in his hands—and now two little soldiers for him to test, to enjoy watching as they pitted their abilities against the remnants of Umbrella's bio-organic weaponry—he was happy. Would they live or die? Either way, he would be satisfied.

"Open the cages, my darlings," he murmured, and began to sing.

EIGHT

Rebecca pushed herself through the air shaft, ignoring the layers of dust and cobwebs that were collecting on her hair and clothes, ignoring the suffocatingly close walls of thin metal. The map only showed the connecting shaft running between two rooms on the basement's first floor, but there were spaces on the second, sub-basement floor that seemed to be part of the system, too. It seemed likely that one of the shafts vented outside. Billy hadn't been overly enthusiastic—*likely* wasn't the same as *probably,* he'd said—but they both agreed that it was worth a shot.

At least it's not very long, she thought, edging toward the square of light not far ahead. There was a thin metal grille covering the exit, but it popped off with a few taps, clattering to the floor below.

She got a quick look at a big stone room, dank and empty in the flicker of a dying light fixture, then pushed herself out, grabbing the edge of the vent and somersaulting to a crouch. She stood up, brushing herself off, taking in the new room.

Oh, jeez. It was like some medieval dungeon, large, gloomy, a cavern made of stone. The rock walls were fixed with chains, the chains fixed with manacles. There were a number of devices sitting around that she didn't recognize, but that could only have been made to inflict pain. There were boards with rusty nails in them, knotted ropes in bunches, and next to a scum-thick broken wall fountain was a large standing case that looked like an iron maiden. She had no doubt that the dark, faded stains in the crevices of the rough-hewn wall were blood.

"Everything okay? Over?"

She picked up her radio. "I don't think 'okay' is the right word," she said. "But I'm all right, over."

"Is there another air shaft, over?"

She turned, searching the walls for a vent—and saw one, twenty feet overhead.

"Yeah, but it's in the ceiling," she said, and sighed. Even if they had a ladder to reach the vent, they couldn't climb straight up. She spotted the room's one door, in the southwest corner. "Where does the door from here lead, over?"

A pause. "Looks like it opens into a small room that leads back into the corridor we came through," he said. "Should I meet you back in the corridor, over?"

Rebecca started for the door. "That makes the most sense. Maybe we can try—"

Before she could complete the sentence, a terrible sound filled the room, like nothing she'd ever heard before but also strangely familiar. It was a high, monkeylike shriek—

—that's it. The primate house, at the zoo.

—that was echoing, howling through the cavernous space, coming from nowhere and everywhere at once. Rebecca looked up just as a pale, long-limbed creature peered out at her from the ceiling vent. It bared its teeth, thick and sharp, clutching the air in front of its muscular chest with limber fingers, screeching horribly.

Before she could take a step, the creature leaped from the vent, jumping off against one rock wall before landing on the floor in a squat, on a tumble of thin boards in the middle of the room. It stared up at her, its lips drawn back over its yellowed teeth. It looked almost like a baboon with short white fur, except that there were great tears in the fur, glistening patches of dense red muscle showing through. It didn't look as though it had been attacked, but rather as though its muscles had grown too large for its skin

143

and were splitting through. Its hands were too big, its nails overly long, and they dragged and ticked across the stone floor as it edged toward her from the pile of boards, grinning maliciously.

Slow . . . Rebecca eased her weapon off her hip, as frightened as she'd been all night. Normal baboons were capable of ripping a person apart, and this one looked like it had been infected.

The baboon edged closer—and from overhead she heard another, at least two other voices begin to shriek, the noise getting louder, more of the sick animals approaching. It was close enough now for her to smell, the hot and musky scent of urine and feces and wildness, of overpowering infection.

"Rebecca! What's going on?"

She still held the radio in her left hand. She depressed the button, afraid to speak but more afraid that Billy's shouting would incite the creature, make it attack.

"Sshhh," she said, her voice soft, as much to calm the animal as to shut Billy up. She took a step back, clipping the radio to the collar of her shirt, raising the nine-millimeter. The baboon squatted lower, tensing its legs—

—and sprang, just as she fired, just as two more lithe and screaming forms hopped and capered into the room from the air shaft, one of them striking her head as it fell past, its ragged nails tearing at her hair. The strike pushed her out of the attacker's way, but it also knocked her off balance, her shot hitting nothing but wall, all of them landing on the pile of boards—

—and then the floor collapsed.

There had been no new developments. The strange young man, whoever he was—and Wesker had his suspicions, which he kept to himself—had not appeared again, nor had the image of James Marcus. The cameras didn't seem to be working correctly, either, making surveillance something of a moot point. Many had simply gone black, leaving them nothing to see, to consider.

After several long, boring moments of listening to Birkin talk about his new virus, Wesker pushed back from the video console and stood up, stretching. It was funny—a few years ago, he might have been interested in his old friend's work. Now, with his own departure from Umbrella's folds looming, he found himself unable even to pretend.

"Well, it's been quite a day," Wesker said, breaking through William's obsessive monologue when he took a breath. "I'll be off."

Birkin stared at him, his pinched, pallid face looming ghostly by the white light of the screens. "What? Where are you going?"

"Home. There's nothing more we can do here."

"But—you said—what about the cleanup?"

Wesker shrugged. "Umbrella will send another team, I'm sure."

"I thought keeping the spills quiet was the most important thing. Didn't you say it was vital?"

"Did I?"

"Yes!" Birkin was actually angry. "I don't want anyone else from Umbrella coming in. They might start asking questions about my work. I need more time."

Wesker shrugged again. "So, set off the auto-destruct yourself, and tell our contact that it's all taken care of."

Birkin nodded, though Wesker could see the uneasiness that flashed through his gaze. Wesker dodged a smile. Birkin was afraid of their newest contact to the big boys at HQ, avoiding interaction when he could. Wesker couldn't blame him. There was something about Trent, his oddly self-possessed nature—

"What about—him?" Birkin nodded toward the screens. Wesker felt a trace of unease himself, but kept his expression unperturbed.

"A fanatic with a grudge. He's great with video tricks, but I imagine he'll burn as well as anyone else." Wesker didn't quite believe that himself, but wasn't interested in unraveling the mystery. He wasn't a detective in some cheap conspiracy novel, driven by a need to get to the bottom of things. In his experience, anomalies tended to resolve themselves, one way or another.

"If word about what really happened to Dr. Marcus were to get out—"

"It won't," Wesker said.

Birkin refused to be placated. "But what about Spencer's estate, the facilities there?"

Wesker started for the door, his boots clanging across the metal mesh. Birkin followed like a wayward pup.

"Leave that to me," he said. "Umbrella wants combat data, I'm going to give it to them. I'll take the S.T.A.R.S. in, see how real training holds up against the B.O.W.s." He smiled, thinking of the talent on the Alpha team. Strongman Barry, Chris's sharpshooting, Jill and her eclectic upbringing, the daughter of an unparalleled thief . . . It would be a most interesting fight. After seeing little Rebecca Chambers in the facility, it was obvious that something untimely had happened to Enrico's team; Wesker could use that, take the Alphas in to "find" the remaining men.

Even if the Bravos manage to get themselves back to civilization, there will be the missing Rebecca to go in search of. The girl was brilliant, but brains didn't equal combat experience. In fact, she was probably dead already.

They left the control room, Wesker striding down

the hall, Birkin jogging to keep up. They reached the elevator, still open from Wesker's arrival, and Wesker stepped inside. Birkin stood facing him, and in the brighter light of the corridor, Wesker could see the taint of insanity in the scientist's face. His eyes were rimmed in darkness, and he'd developed a facial tic at one corner of his mouth. Wesker wondered vaguely if Annette had noticed her husband's descent into the deeper wells of paranoia, then decided that she probably hadn't. That woman was blind to everything but the "greatness" of her husband's work. Unfortunate for their daughter, to have such parents.

"I'll set the destruct sequence," Birkin said.

"Time it for morning," Wesker said, flashing a grin. "The dawn of a new day."

The doors closed on Birkin's determined expression, a look of resolve on the face of a sheep, and Wesker's grin widened, his heart light with thoughts of what was to come. Everything was about to change, for all of them.

"Billy, help!"

Billy was running as soon as he heard the animal shrieks, the crash, and was in the corridor when Rebecca's frightened shout crackled from the radio. He ran faster, stuffing the maps in his back pocket, his weapon in hand, cursing himself for letting her go through the air shaft.

There, straight ahead, was the door, not far from one of the giant spider bodies. He barreled into it, slamming against it with one shoulder as he grabbed the latch and lifted. The door crashed open and he was through. The overhead fluorescents strobed, damaged, giving the room an unreal air, some kind of lab, maybe, though there was a mildewed cot in one corner. *Doesn't matter, go!*

He flew across the room to the next door, Rebecca shouting again, calling for him to watch out, to hurry. As he pushed at the latch, he caught a movement off to one side, turned and saw a decrepit-looking zombie standing in a corner. The lights buzzed on and off, the dying man watching him silently, his ravaged form disappearing into darkness with each flicker. It began to shuffle toward him.

Later, buddy. Billy flung the second door open, ran inside.

Almost immediately, something flew at him, screaming. He ducked, caught a confused blur of red and white, of animal stink, and then the creature—it was a monkey, some kind of monkey—was past him, still screaming. It was joined by two others, the three of them quickly forming a loose circle around Billy, their lanky, muscular arms and legs in constant motion, swiping at him, their diseased-looking bodies dancing closer to him, then away. He backed up, wedged himself into the corner where the door met a rock wall, not wanting to be cornered but more afraid of having his back exposed. The monkeys continued to dance in and out, shrieking.

"Rebecca!" he shouted.

"Down here!"

She sounded far away. He saw the hole then, a few meters away. Pieces of splintered board littered the floor around it. He couldn't see her at all.

"Hang on," he called, and turned his full attention to the monkeys just as one of them got in close enough to make contact.

It swiped at him with one overly large paw, its talons raking across the tops of his thighs. It didn't break skin but the next hit surely would. Billy didn't aim, just pointed and fired—

—and the monkey spun back, howling, a gout of dark blood erupting from its chest, but it wasn't dead, it shook its head, stepped forward again, and Billy thought that he was probably screwed, they were too powerful, too organized. He couldn't get any one of them without opening himself to attack—

—except both of the others leaped on the wounded third, tearing into it with greedy hands. The injured animal screamed, struggling, but its blood had inspired a feeding frenzy, the other two ripping it apart in seconds, stuffing great wet chunks of its flesh into their mouths.

Billy had time to aim, and took it. One, two,

three shots, and the monkeys were down, dead or dying.

He ran to the hole, dropped to his knees and scurried to the ragged edge, his heart pounding—then sinking, as he saw how far down she was. She was hanging onto a piece of metal piping with both hands, a full floor *beneath* where he was standing. Beyond that, darkness gaped. It was impossible to know how far she might fall.

"Billy," she gasped, looking up at him with frightened eyes.

"Don't let go," he said, and snatched the maps from his pocket, scanning for her position, for the fastest way to get to her. There was no quick access to the basement's second floor, not from the first. He'd have to go back through the lobby, probably through that dining room door where he'd seen the zombies. The stairs to the sub-basement were on the east side of the house.

"I don't know how long I can hold on," she breathed. Her whisper was magnified through her radio, through his. She'd activated an open channel at some point.

"Don't you *dare* let go," he said. "That's a goddamn *order*, little girl, you got it?"

She didn't reply, but he saw her jaw tighten. *Good,* maybe pissing her off would keep her strong. He was already on his feet again.

"I'm coming," he said, and turned and ran, back through the door to the strobe-light lab. The zombie there had moved, was standing in between him and the room's exit back to the corridor, but Billy didn't bother with the weapon, too afraid for Rebecca to take the time. He put out one arm like a quarterback in the big game and hurtled into the creature, shoving as hard as he could, still running as the zombie reeled back, fell to the floor. Billy was out and gone before its frustrated, hungry cry could reach him.

Down the hall, past the impossible spiders, up the stairs. He ejected the clip in the nine-millimeter, pocketed it, fumbled the spare out and jammed it home as he tore through the lobby. *Hang on, hang on . . .*

He didn't hesitate at the dining room door, slamming it open, rushing inside. He spotted two of the zombies safely out of his way, blocked by the dining room table. The third was standing near the door he thought would lead him to Rebecca, it was the soldier with the fork in his shoulder, and Billy stopped just long enough to take aim, to fire two rounds into its already oozing head. The first went wide, but the second shot blew a substantial piece of bone out the back of its skull, painting the wall behind it with rotten gray matter. It hung there a moment, the body, and Billy was already past it by the time it hit the floor.

Through the door, which opened into a short hall. *Left or right?* Without a map of the first floor he couldn't know, but the placement of the stairs on the basement map suggested left. With no time to reason it out he hurried on, leading with his weapon, down a few steps and around a giant, hissing boiler. Steam clouded the maintenance room, but he found his way, found another set of stairs, metal and rusted.

At the bottom was a door. He pushed through, remembering from the map that he would enter a large room with some kind of fountain in the middle, something big and round, anyway. There were two smaller rooms to the west, branched off from another short hall, and one of them should be where Rebecca was, *the one all the way at the end, maybe—*

The big room was cold and damp, the walls and floor made of stone. He ran through, glancing at a large monument to his left, what he'd thought was a fountain on the map. It was some kind of statuary. Blind eyes stared at him from the faces of carved animals, watching him sprint by—

—and there was a shriek from the hall just ahead, a blind corner, but he knew the sound from only a minute before: There was another monkey there. Shit! He'd have to take it out, couldn't risk turning his back on it—

"Billy—please—"

The voice over the radio was desperate, and Billy

put on speed, ignoring the part of him that com-
manded him to stop, to wait for the animal to show itself so that he could dispatch it from a safe distance.
He dashed ahead, around the corner, and there was
the monkey, terrible, shredded-looking, howling—

—and Billy, who'd run track in high school,
leaped. He hurdled over it and came down only two
steps from a door, *the* door, the monkey shrieking in
anger behind him. If the door was locked, he was in
trouble, but it wasn't. He bolted through, slamming
it behind him, dropping and skidding on his knees to
the great hole in the floor.

She was there, still there, hanging on with only
one hand now, and he could see that she was slipping.
He dropped his handgun and shot out his arm, grasping her wrist even as her whitened fingertips let go.

"Got you," he panted. "I got you."

Rebecca started to cry as he rocked back on his
heels, lifting her out of the hole, feeling a satisfaction that he'd almost forgotten had existed after all
those months in jail—the sure, easy knowledge that
he'd done the right thing, and done it well.

Billy pulled her out of the hole, using his body as
leverage, pulling her practically on top of him in a
rough embrace. Instead of pushing away, she let him
hold her a moment, clinging to him, unable to stop
the tears of gratitude, of relief. He seemed to under-

stand what she needed, and held her tightly. She'd been so sure that she was going to fall, to die, lost and forgotten in some stinking basement, her corpse picked over by diseased animals . . .

After a moment she rolled off him, wiping at her face with one shaking hand. They both sat on the floor, Billy looking around at the bleak rock walls of another nondescript basement chamber, Rebecca looking at Billy. When the silence stretched too long, she reached out, put a hand on his arm.

"Thank you," she said. "You saved my life. Again."

He glanced at her, looked away. "Yeah, well. We have that truce thing, you know?"

"Yeah, I know," she said. "And I also know you're not a killer, Billy. Why were you on your way to Ragithon? Did you—were you really involved in those murders?"

He met her gaze evenly. "You could say that," he said. "I was there, anyway."

I was there . . . That wasn't the same thing as actually killing anyone. "I don't think you killed your escort earlier tonight; I think it was one of these creatures, and you just ran," she said. "And I know I haven't known you for very long, but I don't believe that you murdered twenty-three people, either."

"It doesn't matter," Billy said, staring at his boots. "People believe what they want to believe."

S.D. Perry

"It matters to me," Rebecca said, her voice gentle. "I'm not going to judge. I just want to know. What happened?"

He was still staring at his boots, but his gaze had gone distant, as if seeing another time, another place. "Last year, my unit was sent to Africa, to intervene in a civil war," he said. "Top secret, no U.S. involvement, you understand. We were supposed to raid a guerrilla hideout. It was summer, the hottest part of summer, and we were dropped well outside the strike zone, in the middle of a dense jungle. We had to hike in a ways . . ."

He trailed off a moment, reaching for his dog tags, holding them tightly. When he spoke again, his voice was even softer. "The heat got half of us. The enemy got most of the rest, picking us off one at a time. By the time we got to where the hideout was supposed to be, there were only four of us left. We were exhausted, half crazy, sick with the heat, sick with—with heartsickness, I guess, watching our buddies die.

"So when we reached the hideout coordinates, we were ready to blow all of them away. Make someone pay, you know? For all that sickness. Only, there was no hideout. The tip-off wasn't valid. It turned out to be some dumpy little village, just a bunch of farmers. Families. Old men and women. Children."

156

Rebecca nodded, encouraging him to go on, but her stomach was starting to knot. There was an inevitability to the story; she could see where it was headed, and it wasn't pretty.

"Our team leader told us to round them up, and we did," Billy said. "And then he told us—"

His voice broke. He reached out and picked up his dropped weapon, stuffing it into his belt almost angrily as he stood up, turning away. Rebecca stood up, too.

"Did you?" she asked. "Did you kill them?"

Billy turned back to her, his lips curled. "What if I tell you that I did? Would you judge me then?"

"Did you?" she asked again, studying his face, his eyes, determined to at least try and understand. And it was as though he could see it in her, could see that she was working to be open to the truth. He stared at her a moment, then shook his head.

"I tried to stop it," he said. "I tried, but they knocked me down. I was barely conscious, but I saw it, I saw it all . . . and I couldn't do anything." He looked away before continuing. "When it was over, when we were picked up, it was their word against mine. There was a trial, sentencing, and—well, then this happened."

He spread his arms, encompassing their surroundings. "So if we make it out of here, I'm dead, anyway. It's that or I run, and keep running."

It all had the ring of truth. If he was lying, he deserved an Oscar . . . And she didn't think he was. She tried to think of something to say, something reassuring, that would make things better somehow, but nothing came. He was right about his options.

"Hey," he said, looking at something past her shoulder. "Check it out."

She turned as he stepped by, saw a stack of scrap metal pieces leaning against the far wall—and half-hidden among them, what looked like a shotgun.

"Is that what I think it is?" she asked.

Billy picked up the weapon, grinning as he pumped it, checking the action. "Yes, ma'am, it certainly is."

"Is it loaded?"

"No, but I have a couple of shells, left from the train. It's a twelve gauge." He smiled again. "Things are looking up. We may not make it, but there's a monkey out in the hall that's just begging for a taste of this baby."

"Actually, I think it's a baboon," she said, surprised to find herself smiling back. Then they were both chuckling, struck by the absolute pointlessness of her correction. They were trapped in an isolated mansion, hunted by God knew how many kinds of monster, but at least they knew that the creature in the hall was probably a baboon. Their chuckles turned to laughter.

She watched him laugh, all pretense of arrogance, of tough-guy machismo set aside, and felt that she was truly seeing him for the first time, the real Billy Coen. She realized in that moment that she had thoroughly failed her first assignment. He was no more her prisoner than she was his. Assuming they survived, if he ran, she wouldn't be able to bring herself to stop him.

So much for a career in law enforcement.

The thought made her laugh even harder.

Nine

The baboon ran for them as soon as they stepped back into the hall—and it died spectacularly, the double-barreled shotgun blasting it to shreds with a deafening roar. Billy broke and reloaded with his one remaining shell. He thought he'd had more, but it seemed he'd lost them somewhere along the way. In any case, nothing else came at them, and they headed back out toward the main room, Billy feeling much lighter than he had in a long time. Besides the much-needed laugh, a break in the relentless chaos they'd both endured, it was the first time he'd told his story to anyone who was actually listening, who was willing to consider that he might be telling the truth.

They stopped at the giant circle of stone statuary

in the middle of the large chamber, looking it over. There were six carved animals spaced evenly around the circle, facing outward. Each had a small plaque in front of it, a small oil lamp positioned next to each plaque. The animals were expertly carved, but the whole thing was a monstrosity, a real eyesore.

The animal in front of him was an eagle in flight, a snake clutched in its talons. He read aloud from its plaque: "I DANCE FREELY THROUGH THE AIR, CAPTURING A LEGLESS PREY." He frowned, moved to the next animal over, a deer, reading from its plaque. "I STAND TALL ON THE EARTH WITH HORNS PROUDLY DISPLAYED."

Rebecca had walked around the unfortunate art piece, stopped at a steel gate set into the wall behind it. The gate blocked a short hall, two doors set into its walls. "There's a sign here, says"—she turned, studying the animals—"basically, go from weakest to strongest, using the lamps. It's some kind of puzzle." She grabbed one of the metal bars of the gate, shook it. "Must be how we open the gate."

"So you have to light the lamps in order, starting with the weakest animal," Billy said. Dumb. Why someone would go through all the trouble . . . He pulled the map out of his back pocket, studied it. "It just looks like a couple of rooms back there. I don't see an exit."

Rebecca shrugged. "Yeah, but maybe there's something in there we can use. Can it hurt?"

"I don't know," he said truthfully. "Maybe."

She smiled, turning to the stone animal nearest her, a tiger, reading from the plaque beneath it. "I AM THE KING OF ALL I SURVEY: NO CREATURE CAN ESCAPE MY GRASP."

Billy moved to his left, to a carving of a snake coiled around a tree limb. "This one says, I CREEP UP ON MY VICTIMS IN LEGLESS SILENCE AND CONQUER EVEN THE MIGHTIEST OF KINGS WITH MY POISON."

Rebecca read the last two aloud—the words beneath a wolf carving were, MY SHARP WIT ALLOWS ME TO BRING DOWN EVEN THE GREATEST HORNED BEAST. The sixth animal was a horse, reared back on its hind legs. The legend beneath it was, NO AMOUNT OF CUNNING CAN MATCH THE SPEED OF MY SUPPLE LIMBS.

Horned beast. Billy walked back to the deer, read the part about "horns proudly displayed."

"So, the wolf is stronger than the deer," he said.

"And if cunning can't outrace a horse, the horse is stronger than the wolf," she said. "What's stronger than the snake?"

"Gotta be the eagle, it's carrying a snake," Billy said.

They each circled around the statue, calling out observations, working the puzzle. They finally agreed on a sequence, and Billy walked to each animal, lighting the appropriate oil lamp in the appropriate order—from weakest to strongest, at least according to the statue, the order was deer, wolf, horse, tiger, snake, and eagle.

As he lit the eagle's lamp, there was a heavy, mechanical sound from somewhere inside the statuary—and the steel gate behind them rose smoothly, sliding into a niche at the top of the archway.

Together, they moved down the hall. The first room, on their right, appeared to hold nothing of value at first glance. There were a bunch of emptied packing crates, a few cluttered shelves. Billy was ready to move on when Rebecca stepped inside, heading for the crates. One of them was turned away from the door so they couldn't see what was in it— and when she stepped around it, she let out an excited laugh, crouching next to the crate, pushing it around so he could see. Billy hurried to her side, feeling like a kid at Christmas. *Guess that damned puzzle was worth the effort, after all.*

Two and a half boxes of nine-millimeter rounds. A half box of twenty-twos, which wouldn't do them much good, nor would the pair of speed loaders— Billy had to explain that the round metal gadgets were designed to quickly load revolvers—with the .50 rounds. But the box of shotgun shells, fourteen in all, would certainly help. Billy wouldn't have minded running across a bazooka, but all things considered, they couldn't have hoped for much better.

They spent a few minutes loading the clips they

had. Rebecca found a fanny pack with a broken zipper on one of the shelves and they loaded it up,
along with her utility belt; they agreed it was better
to take it all, on the chance that they might discover
more weapons. Billy rigged the zipper with a safety
pin he found on the floor and donned the pack, comforted by the weight of so much ammo.

"I could kiss you," he said, lifting the shotgun—
and at her silence, he turned to look at her, saw that
she'd flushed slightly. She looked away, adjusting
her belt.

"I didn't mean literally," he said. "I mean, not that
you're not attractive, but you're—I'm—I meant—"

"Don't have kittens," she said coolly. "I know
what you meant."

Billy nodded, relieved. They had enough to deal
with without the male-female thing. *Though she is
pretty cute—*

He shook it off, reminding himself that he'd just
spent a year without any women around—and now
was *so* not the time to address it.

They headed to the second door, found it unlocked. It was a bunk room, shabby and dirty, the
bunks slapped together from plywood, the few blan-
kets scattered around threadbare and dingy. Considering the poor accommodations and the locked steel
gate down the hall, Billy thought it was safe to assume that the inhabitants hadn't been volunteers. Re-

becca had told him what that diary had said, about testing human subjects . . .

The whole facility gave him the creeps. The sooner they could get out, the better.

"Do we go down, or up?" Rebecca asked, as they moved back into the hall.

"There's an observatory upstairs, right?" Billy asked. Rebecca nodded. "So let's go observe. Maybe we can signal for help or something."

He realized that he'd just suggested they try and get rescued, but he didn't take it back, even understanding what it most likely meant for him. He knew that he'd rather die fighting for his life than be executed . . . But there was Rebecca to consider. She was a good person, honest and sincere, and he'd do what he could to get her out of this alive.

They moved out, Billy wondering where his criminal nature had gotten off to, quickly deciding that he was better off without it. For the first time since that terrible day in the jungle village, he felt like himself again.

He watched them stock up on ammunition, both impressed and disappointed by their fortitude. After another consultation with their maps, they started upstairs, presumably for the observatory; although the children could hear their voices, they could not make out their words.

He'd had the children search out the tablets that would be needed, had had the tablets taken to the doors that led to the observatory. Unless Billy and Rebecca were entirely moronic—which they'd already proven they were not—they would figure out how to trigger the structure's rotation, leading them closer to their escape. From there they would move on to the laboratory, hidden behind the chapel . . .

He wondered what they would find there, in Marcus's laboratories; more to steal, perhaps. He wanted them to uncover what they could about Umbrella's true nature, but was not pleased to see them picking through the sad remnants of Marcus's brilliant career.

He still thought of the laboratories as Marcus's, though Marcus had been gone for a decade. The entire complex had been shut down after the manager's "disappearance," but recently, Umbrella had reopened it all—the labs, the treatment plant, the training center. None had been fully functional when the virus had hit; they were being run by skeleton crews of maintenance men, watched over by a handful of middle management hopefuls; nonetheless, the company had lost a number of loyal employees.

Billy and Rebecca moved through the east rooms on the first floor and back out into the lobby, then headed to the second floor. They found the door that would take them to the third easily enough, entering the stairwell with weapons drawn, their youthful faces determined and seemingly unafraid. He watched as they started up the stairs, emotionally torn. He wanted to see them succeed, *and* see them die. Was there a way to have both? They had managed the Eliminator series easily, although the primates had been weakened by hunger and neglect. How would they fare against the Hunters? Or the proto-Tyrant?

What if they came to where he and the children waited and watched? What would they do?

The young man frowned, unhappy with the thought. Sensitive to his moods, a number of the many slid up his legs, across his chest, gathering in a kind of embrace. He pet them, reassured them by touch that all was well. If the two adventurers actually made it to the nest—still an unlikely premise— he would let them pass, of course, so that they might spread the story of Umbrella's sins.

"Or perhaps I'll kill them," he said, shrugging. He would decide when—if—it occurred. To say that he was indifferent to their fate was untrue; as he waited for the death of Umbrella to unfold, watching Billy and Rebecca had become a pleasure, and he was most interested to see what would happen to them. But he would see them dead before he'd let them hurt the children again.

They had reached the top of the stairs, were cautiously peering around the railing, searching for movement. The young man suddenly remembered the Centurion, hiding in the walls of the breeding pool, and wondered if it would come out to see who had invaded its territory. Billy and Rebecca had best hope not. If the Eliminators were but pawns in this game, the Centurion was one of his knights. The young man eagerly leaned in to watch.

The trip up to the third floor had been uneventful, though they'd had to hurry through the dining room; the two zombies that roamed around the tables had been too slow to bother shooting, but she didn't feel particularly comfortable taking a leisurely stroll past the dying creatures, either. Considering that Billy was three steps ahead of her, he obviously felt the same.

Now, standing at the top of the stairs, Rebecca relaxed a little. The third floor—at least this part of it—was a single, giant room, no hidden corners to worry about. The doors to the observatory were over to their right. Straight across from them was the breeding pool, a recessed, empty pit that stretched most of the room's length, and to the left, a door that, according to the map, led to an outdoor patio.

"What do you think they were breeding?" Billy asked, his voice low. Still, it echoed slightly in the vast room.

"Don't know. Leeches, maybe," she said. She thought about that solitary figure they'd seen from the train, singing to the leeches, and suppressed a shudder. "So, observatory or patio?"

Billy looked back and forth, then shrugged. "It seems safe. We could each take one door—just open and look, though, no splitting up, okay?"

Rebecca nodded. She definitely felt safer having a bigger supply of ammo, but that fall had knocked some caution into her. She wasn't nearly so gung-ho on separating. "I'll take the patio."

They moved out, their footsteps echoing in the huge chamber. The door to the observatory was closer; only her steps rang out after a moment, as she continued on to the south wall.

"Hey," Billy called, as she reached the door. He was holding up what looked like a book, two more in his other hand. Rebecca squinted across the large room, saw that they were made of stone, that each was rounded on one end. "These were in front of the door."

"What are they?" she said. Her voice, though low, carried easily in the still, cool air.

"Decorative, maybe," he said. "Each one has a word etched on the front." He looked down at the tablets, shuffled through them. "Ah . . . we got unity, discipline, and obedience."

That recording they'd heard, Dr. Marcus's recitation of the company motto—they were the same three words. "Hang on to 'em," Rebecca said. "They might be part of some puzzle, like the animals."

"My thoughts exactly," Billy said, and in a lower voice, "crazy-ass house."

She turned back to the door, raising her handgun as she pushed at the handle—and it was locked. She sighed, her shoulders sagging, realizing how amped up she'd been for some kind of attack.

"Locked," she called out.

Billy had opened the door to the observatory and was still looking inside. He turned back, holding the door open. "This might be promising. I don't know what any of it does, but there's a shitload of equipment in here; maybe a radio, too."

A radio. She felt her hopes surge. "Here I—"

The word *come* was cut off by a sound of animal movement, a heavy rattle that reverberated through the room. She and Billy both stared at one another, the distance between them suddenly much greater than she'd previously thought.

The sound came again. It was the sound of something hard rapidly clattering against rock, like someone drumming steel fingers against a tabletop, and it was loud. Whatever it was, it was big—and getting closer, from the increase in sound. It was hard to tell where it was coming from; the echoes masked the direction—

"The breeding pool," Billy shouted, waving her over. "Come on!"

She broke into a run, her heart hammering, afraid to look at the breeding pool, afraid not to. She sensed movement there, something dark and fluid, and ran faster, finally risking a glance as she passed it by.

The sight of it drove conscious thought away. It was a centipede or millipede, big enough to put those shepherd-sized spiders to shame. Yellow eyes seemed to glow from either side of a glossy black skull, long, reddish antennae twitching and quivering from the top of its head. Its long, sinuous body was low to the ground, plated and segmented, riding atop dozens of pointed red legs. It was easily four meters long, maybe longer, as big around as a barrel—and moving toward her, fast, its legs waving, rippling as it propelled itself across the empty pool.

"Run!" Billy yelled, and Rebecca ran for her life, now breathing in the stink of the creature, a terrible sour smell that would have made her gag if she'd had time to bother. Billy was holding the door to the observatory open with his foot, the shotgun trained just past her, and she could *feel* how close it was, feel it like a shadow overtaking her.

Just as she reached Billy, he fired, pumping the shotgun and firing again as she flew past him, diving through the door. The second she was through, he leaped back, the door slamming closed—and a split-second past that, they heard its body brush past the door, the sound of its armored body pressing against heavy wood. They waited, both of them staring at the door—but after a few seconds the sound stopped, became the clatter of many feet moving away.

"Good Christ," Billy said. Rebecca nodded. He reached down, helped her to her feet, both of them breathing heavily.

"Let's not go back that way," Rebecca said, hoping very much that they wouldn't have to.

"Sounds like a plan," Billy agreed.

They were silent for a moment, looking around at their sanctuary. It was a big, round room, bi-level. They were standing on a kind of catwalk that half-circled the room; another set of doors was at the northern end. Near the doors was a short ladder off the walk, leading down to a metal mesh platform that was lined with equipment. Beneath the platform was darkness.

Together, they moved around the walk, stopping at the second set of doors. Locked. They exchanged a dismal glance but said nothing, heading for the ladder. Rebecca went down first, stopping at the large piece of machinery that dominated the room at its center, presumably the telescope. There was a telescope arm, but it was high overhead, out of reach. Behind her, Billy was looking at the rest of the equipment, computer banks and other machines that

she didn't recognize. She turned back to the telescope, looking down at the console—and felt her
breath catch. There were three empty depressions on
it, each shaped like a small tombstone, flat on one
end, rounded on the other.

"I don't see a radio here, but—" Billy was saying,
until she interrupted.

"Tell me you still have those tablets," she said.

Billy turned, looked at the console as he unzipped
his pack. He pulled the tablets out, each about the
size of a paperback book but thinner. Rebecca took
them, remembering Umbrella's discomfiting motto
as she set them in place. "Obedience breeds discipline. Discipline breeds unity. Unity breeds
power . . ."

"And power is life," Billy finished.

As soon as the third tablet fell into place, a giant
sound filled the tall room, a sound of vast machines
at work—and they could feel the room around them
start to descend, like an elevator. Not just the platform, the entire *room,* walls and all. Beneath their
feet, the darkness rose up, became a pool of water,
agitated into a froth by the moving platform. Rebecca had a second to wonder if the platform was
going to stop, a flash of panic that they were about to
be drowned—and then the sound of machinery died
away, the room becoming still again. In the last, fading drone of the machines, they heard a clear *click*

sound coming from the northern doors overhead.

They looked at each other, and Rebecca saw her surprise mirrored on his lean face.

"Guess we know where to go next," Billy said, trying a smile, but it wasn't a convincing one. Rebecca didn't even try. They were being led—but was it to freedom, or like lambs to slaughter?

One way to find out. Without speaking, they turned and walked to the ladder.

✝Еп

They stepped through the northern doors into cool night air, and Billy felt a real sense of relief, breathing deeply. He hadn't realized how afraid he'd been that they might never leave the Umbrella facility. Unfortunately, he quickly saw that they hadn't escaped, not exactly; the doors from the observatory had opened onto a long and narrow walk, leading straight to another building, perhaps fifty meters ahead. The walk was bordered on either side by water, some kind of reservoir or lake that abutted the east side of the facility.

They moved away from the observatory, then turned back to look at where they'd been, spending a few minutes trying to figure out where they were in relation to the lobby, to the rooms they'd seen. It was a lost cause. Billy had never had much of a sense of direction, and it seemed that Rebecca didn't, either. They finally gave up, turning their attention to the tall, foreboding-looking building at the other end of the path.

They walked toward it, Billy still taking in big lungfuls of the sweet, misty air. It was late, probably in the early hours of morning, but there was no sky to judge by, only a great, gray cloak of rain clouds overhead.

"Where do you think we are?" he asked.

"No idea," Rebecca answered. "Somewhere with a phone, I hope."

"And a kitchen," Billy added. He was starving.

"Yeah," she agreed, her tone wistful. "Stocked with pizza and ice cream."

"Pepperoni?"

"Hawaiian," she said. "And pistachio ice cream."

"Gaah." Billy made a face, enjoying the conversation. They hadn't had much time to get to know each other, though he felt a kind of bond with her, the connection he'd often felt for others during combat. "You probably like orange food, too."

"Orange food?"

"Yeah, you know. That unnatural orange color. They put it in macaroni and cheese, artificially flavored orange drinks, snack cakes, fried cheese curls . . ."

"Rebecca grinned. "Got me. I love that stuff."

Billy rolled his eyes. "Teenagers . . . You are a teenager, aren't you?"

"Just old enough to vote," she said, sounding slightly defensive. Before he could ask how she'd made it into S.T.A.R.S. at her age, she added, "I'm one of those brilliant whiz kid types, college grad and everything. And how old are you, grandpa? Thirty?"

It was Billy's turn to feel slightly defensive. "Twenty-six."

She laughed. "Wow, that's ancient. Let me get you a wheelchair."

"Shut up," he said, grinning.

"I said, *let me get you a wheelchair!*" she mock-shouted, cracking him up entirely. They were still laughing when they passed a small, open guardhouse set into the right side of the walkway, and saw the body on the floor inside.

Part of a body, thought Billy, his good mood drying up in a hurry as they stopped, helpless not to look. The legs and one arm were missing, making the face-down corpse look as though he—or she, it was too far gone to tell—was drowning in the thick puddle of blood that surrounded it.

Neither of them spoke again as they finished their walk to the building, sobered by the reminder of the tragedy that had occurred here. It was impossible to keep it in mind every second; dwelling on the horror of the viral outbreak would make it too hard to function, and the occasional release of laughter was important, even necessary, to their continued mental health. On the other hand, if you could look at the body of a dead man and keep laughing, mental health became an issue in an entirely different way.

They reached the unknown structure, slowing, studying the layout. There were small paths branching off of the main walk just in front of the building, hemmed in with flowers and trees that had long since gone to seed, the paths disappearing behind roughly shaped hedges. There were a few unbroken outdoor lights, but only enough to make the shadows seem even darker. Not the most inviting environment, but Billy didn't see any zombies or leech people, which made it a hell of a lot better than the last place.

There were a few wide stone steps leading up to the double doors. Billy kept his eye on the shadowy paths as Rebecca walked up the steps, giving the doors a shake.

"Locked," she said.

"Hell with that," Billy said, following her up. He tried the handle himself, decided that while the wood was strong, the lock wasn't. Not even a deadbolt. "Stand back."

He turned to one side, lowered his center of gravity, and gave the lock a solid side kick, then another. On the third, he heard wood splintering, and it crashed open on the fifth, the cheap metal lock flying apart.

They both stepped into the doorway, looking inside. After all they'd been through, he thought he was past surprise, but he was wrong. It was a church, as ornate as any he'd seen, from the stained glass set high in the wall behind the altar to the gleaming wooden pews. It was also wrecked; at least half the pews were overturned, and they could only see inside because of the giant hole in the ceiling not far from where they stood.

"Look at the altar," Rebecca whispered.

Billy nodded. Not so much the altar itself as what was around it. On the platform at the front of the church were hundreds of burned down candles, tipped-over statues of religious icons, many of them broken or blackened with ash, and great bunches of dead flowers. It was, in a word, creepy.

"I'm okay with getting out of here," Billy said, raising his voice slightly when he realized that he, too, was whispering. "We should check out the grounds, see where some of those paths go."

Rebecca nodded, stepping back—and then something huge and black was swooping down toward them from the high, vaulted ceiling, something that emitted an incredibly high-pitched squeal, that fluttered and darted and flapped giant dusty wings. Time slowed to a crawl, long enough for Billy to get a clear look at it. It was some kind of a bat, but much, much bigger than any he'd ever heard of. The thing had the wingspan of a condor, easy.

It pulled up at the last instant, flew manically back into the darkness overhead, but had come close enough for a wave of its rotten-meat breath to wash over them. Billy pushed Rebecca back with one arm, grabbing at the broken handles of the doors with the other. He jerked them closed, wishing now that he hadn't forced them open, realizing only a second later that it didn't matter. They could hear the massive bat as it pushed its way through the hole in the roof, could hear its giant, ratty claws scrabbling at the shingles.

"Go!" Billy yelled.

They ran down the steps, Rebecca leading them to the right. There was more protection there, part of the pathway that skirted the building covered. It turned sharply, once, twice, the turns hidden by overgrown bushes and plants. Rebecca was fast, but Billy kept up, more than a little motivated by the image of those leathery, fluttering wings enfolding him, those claws piercing his flesh—

"There!" Rebecca slowed, pointed.

To the right of the path just ahead was what looked like an elevator, of all things, free-standing at the side of the church. Billy wasn't sure it was their best bet, but they could clearly hear the beat of wings overhead somewhere, the fiercely high squeal of the bat searching for prey. He followed Rebecca to the door, silently thanking God when the doors slid open to her touch. It was small, barely room for two; they shoved inside, saw that it only went down. Just as well; Billy had no desire to visit the church's belfry, see if the mad bat had any brothers or sisters.

Rebecca hit the switch to close the doors. Just before they closed, a zombie staggered toward them from seemingly out of nowhere, a woman, reaching toward them with fingers that were shredded to the bone. She moaned, revealing blackened teeth, and then the doors were sliding closed, shutting out the zombie, shutting out the high frequency screech of the infected bat.

They both sagged, leaning against the walls of the small elevator. They could hear the female zombie's hungry cries through the doors, hear the sharp scratch of her bone fingertips against the metal doors. Within a few seconds, her low, gravelly moans were joined by another voice, then a third, all of them wailing in eagerness, in frustration.

There were only two choices, B1 or B2. Billy looked at Rebecca, who shook her head, her face pale. Outside, the zombies continued to claw for entry, and Billy pushed B1. The elevator didn't move.

"Okay, B2, then," Billy said, hoping that they hadn't just trapped themselves. He punched the button. The elevator started with a lurch, then descended smoothly. Billy edged slightly in front of Rebecca, readying the shotgun, hoping that the doors weren't about to open to a horde of infected creatures, all eager for a late-night snack.

The doors slid open without any sound, revealing a corridor littered with rubble, but otherwise empty. He pushed the button for B1 again, hoping for another option, but the elevator doors didn't even close. Apparently, they could either go back to the bat and the zombies or they could explore the second basement level. Billy opted for exploration.

He stepped out cautiously, Rebecca right behind. Like the training facility mansion, the decor, the architecture, was refined and probably priceless. The floor was marble, chipped but still polished to a high sheen, the hall lined with handsome support pillars, the entries high and arched. To their left was a stairwell that led up, choked with broken rock and shattered drywall. There was another door on the left up ahead, just before the corridor turned sharply to the right.

They paused at the stairwell but it was a lost cause, the debris piled floor to ceiling. If they wanted to go back up, it was the elevator or nothing . . . though at the moment, Billy did not want to go back up. It seemed like the constant barrage of disgusting, dangerous, frightening creatures would never end, and he was more than ready for a break.

"All those in favor of no more monsters," he said softly.

"Aye," Rebecca answered, her tone just as soft. She shot him a smile, but it looked strained. They started forward, boots crunching as they waded through the rubble.

Rebecca stayed by the first door as Billy quickly checked the rest of the corridor. There was one other obvious door, set with a combination lock—and a third possible door: Billy wasn't sure, it looked very much like the corridor simply dead-ended in a blue wall, but there was an elaborate shrine set up there—twin statues bookended a profiled relief of someone who looked very much like James Marcus. There was no keyhole, but beneath the bust was an empty depression the size of a child's fist, as though it were missing a piece.

Lovely. Two more puzzle locks, Billy thought sourly, walking back to Rebecca. What was it with these people? If they needed to be so goddamn clever, why couldn't they just stick to crossword puzzles?

Thankfully, the first door was unlocked. They stepped inside, finding themselves in another shabbily elegant room, this one lined with bookshelves. A stained oriental rug lay on the floor in the room's first section. The room itself was vaguely u-shaped. There were several lamps on, making it the brightest room they'd been in all night, and besides the shelves, there were several low tables and a small desk with an antique typewriter. Billy walked to the nearest desk, picked up a scrap of paper.

" 'Trouble is unlikely, but I've taken precautions,' " he read. " 'To hide a leaf, put it in the forest. To hide a key, make it look like a leaf.' "

"Gee, that clears things up," Rebecca said, and Billy nodded. Again—what was it with these people?

Rebecca looked the shelves over while Billy walked the room, noting a large hole in the ceiling around the corner from the door. It was high, but using one of the tables . . .

"Most of these are biology," Rebecca called. "Mammalian, insectile, amphibian . . ."

"Come look at this," Billy called back. As she stepped around the corner, Billy grabbed the nearest table, pushing it under the hole. He still wouldn't be able to reach . . .

"I could go up," Rebecca said. "Look around, find a rope or something for you to climb."

Billy frowned. "I don't know. Last time you went looking . . ."

"Yeah," she said, but her expression was set. She

was willing, if not eager—and they had to do something.

Billy stepped on the table, interlacing his fingers to give her a boost. She climbed up after him, put her right boot in his hands, one hand on his shoulder. As before, she was light as a feather; Billy could probably bench press two of her without much trouble. He pushed her up easily, Rebecca disappearing from sight as she crawled through. A second later, she was back at the hole.

"Seems clear, but it's dark," she said. "Looks like a lab room, lot of shelves, couple of desks . . . Let me see what I can find."

She disappeared again. Billy waited, staring up at the hole, reminding himself that she knew how to handle herself. She'd already proven herself stronger and more capable than any number of seasoned soldiers he'd known—and if there was trouble, she could just hop back down, nothing to worry about—

Rebecca let out a short, sharp scream and Billy's blood went cold.

"Rebecca!" he shouted, his gaze fixed helplessly on the dark hole overhead.

It looked like a lab, one that had only been used intermittently in the last decade, and hadn't been cleaned at all in that time. There was thick dust on the floor and shelves, but things had been moved at some point, leaving signs—tracks behind chairs, fingerprints on specimen bottles. Rebecca took a quick look at her immediate surroundings, then leaned back over the hole. Billy's expression was tense, expectant.

"Seems clear, but it's dark. Looks like a lab room, lot of shelves, couple of desks . . . Let me see what I can find."

She turned, surveyed the small room again—and realized that it was bigger than she thought, part of it hidden behind a large shelf that bisected the area. She wouldn't have noticed if not for the faint, pale, bluish light that seemed to be emanating from the hidden section. Holding her nine-millimeter, she stepped around the corner—

—and yelped, almost firing at the glowing, floating monster in front of her before she realized that it wasn't alive.

"Rebecca!"

"I'm okay!" she called back, staring at the bizarre creature. "Got a surprise, is all. Hang on."

She stepped closer to the human-sized specimen tube, filled with clear liquid, lit from inside. There were actually four of the tubes, all in a row, each containing a slightly different horror than the one before. The things inside had been human, once, but they had been surgically altered, and almost certainly infected with T-virus. She tried to think of some description to give Billy, but they defied description; grossly misshapen limbs hung from muscular, patchwork bodies, the nearly unrecognizable faces wearing bizarre expressions of anguish and bloodlust. They were horrifying.

Past the row of humanoid monstrosities was a specimen case, filled with much smaller tubes. Rebecca leaned in, saw that each tube had a dead leech inside. She grimaced, was about to turn away—when she realized that one of the tubes was different. The leech inside was . . . not a leech.

She pushed the dusty glass door aside and pulled out the anomalous tube, holding it up to the faint light. The tube's cap was glued or soldered shut, and the thing inside was leech shaped, but was sculpted or carved, and a deep, cobalt blue.

Why would anyone make a fake leech and then put it—

She blinked, remembering that piece of paper Billy had read from—to hide a leaf, put it in the forest. To hide a key . . .

Rebecca walked back to the hole, held the tube out for Billy to see. "I think I found the leaf key," she said, and tossed it down. "Or I guess I should say *leech* key."

Billy caught it neatly, peered at it. "I'm pretty sure it'll fit one of those doors," he said. "Come back down, we can go check."

"The cap won't come off—" she started, stopping

as Billy dropped the tube on the floor next to the table. He grinned up at her, then jumped down, stomping the tube with the heel of his boot. Glass crinkled and crunched, and a second later, he was holding the carving up.

"Not a problem," he said. "Come on."

She chewed at her lip, looking around the lab. There were file cabinets, papers lying around . . .

"You go check. I'm going to see if I can find another map."

Billy frowned. "You sure?"

"Afraid to go by yourself?" she called, smiling slightly.

"Frankly, yes," he said, but smiled back. "Okay. I'll be back in a minute. Don't wander too far away, all right? If you need anything, give me a call."

Rebecca tapped her radio. "No sweat."

He gazed up at her another moment, then turned and walked away. Rebecca looked around the lab once more, focusing on the larger of the two desks in the room. "Okay, Marcus, let's see if you left us anything useful," she said, and moved to the desk, unaware that she was being watched very, very closely as she picked up a sheaf of papers and started to read.

This will not do.

He clenched his fists, furious. The children tried

to soothe him, crawled across his shoulders, but he brushed them away, ignored their attempts.

Rebecca, reading Dr. Marcus's personal notes. Finding the charm that led to Dr. Marcus's inner sanctum, giving it to Billy. All they had to do was get to the cable car, perhaps pick a lock or two, and they could be on their way . . . But it seemed they would not leave the memory of Dr. Marcus alone, that they had to violate the very few privacies he'd left behind.

"Not if we stop them," he told the children, watching as Billy used the small effigy to open Dr. Marcus's rooms, as Rebecca rifled carelessly through Marcus's private papers. It had been an amusing diversion, watching these two, but it was over now. The world would have to learn the truth about Umbrella without them.

Time to send the children out to play.

Eleven

As he'd suspected, that dead end shrine *was* a door, and the tiny leech statue that Rebecca had found fit perfectly in the door's "lock." There was a soft, hidden *click* and the door unlatched.

Billy studied the front of the door a moment before going in, deciding that the profile was, in fact, that of Dr. James Marcus. He wondered why the leech man they'd seen on the train had looked like Marcus; the leeches had been controlled by that obviously much younger man, the one singing outside. Was the real Marcus still around? It didn't seem likely. That diary Rebecca had found—Marcus had been raving, paranoid that Spencer was coming for him, coming to take his work, and that had been ten years ago. People that nuts usually weren't able to hold down day jobs.

Rebecca was waiting. He set the minor mystery aside and pushed past the extravagant door with the barrel of the shotgun. A quick scan for movement—nothing—and he lowered the weapon, stepping farther inside.

"Wow," he said, hushed, looking around the room. It was an office, large, expensively fitted with built-in shelves and cabinets on one side, all dark, polished wood and beveled glass, an ornate fireplace opposite. The antique wood furniture—a low table, chairs, a big desk—was beautiful, the carpet plush, silencing his steps. He saw a door at the back of the room, behind the desk, and mentally crossed his fingers that it would turn out to be their escape route.

Much of the room's light came from a huge aquarium that dominated the northeast corner near where he stood, painting everything with watery bluish light, though the aquarium itself was empty—

—Billy frowned, stepped closer. Not empty. There were no fish, no rocks or plants, but there were a number of things floating at the top—disgusting things, unrecognizable but no less grotesque. They appeared to be pieces of human flesh, but shapeless, boneless, like deformed, amputated body parts. Billy quickly moved on, disturbed by the pale floating objects.

One of the wall cabinets stood open, and Billy walked to it, scanning the books inside. An ancient photo album lay on one shelf and he picked it up. He knew he had to get back to Rebecca but he was curious, wondering if the bust on the door meant he was in Marcus's office.

The photos were old, yellowed and curled. He turned a few pages, decided it was a waste of time. He started to put the album back—and a loose picture fluttered out. He stooped to pick it up, held it up to the blue, rippling light.

The picture itself wasn't particularly interesting, a trio of young men from the thirties or forties, all looking clean-cut and well scrubbed, smiling at the picture taker. On the back, someone had written, "To James, To commemorate your graduation, 1939."

Billy studied the photo, decided that the young man in the middle could be James Marcus. Something about the shape of the head . . . He looked familiar, somehow . . .

"That guy," he said, nodding to himself. The singer from the train. They hadn't seen him well, but he had the same stance, the same wide shoulders . . . "He could be Marcus's son. Or grandson."

There was a puzzle here, and he was starting to think he'd just found another piece. If Spencer had overthrown Marcus, taken his work, wouldn't Marcus's son, or his son's son, want revenge? Maybe the viral outbreak hadn't been an accident. Maybe the guy with the leeches had done it.

Billy sighed, setting the photo on top of the album. That was all good and well, but for all practical purposes, who gave a shit? He needed to be looking for a way out.

He checked the desk for keys or maps, found nothing, and went to the room's second door, thankfully unlocked. He pushed it open, felt his hopes dwindle; there was no big tunnel with a flashing exit sign. It was an art storage room, looked like, paintings stacked against walls, a few statues draped with sagging dropcloths. One statue was uncovered, a white marble piece that looked like one of those old Roman gods, seated against one flocked wall, its dusty gaze uplifted, a hand cupped near its belly—

—and holding something. Something green.

Billy walked over and took the small object from the statue's pallid fingers, smiling faintly when he realized what it was. It was another carving of a leech, this one in green instead of blue.

Another key, perhaps to another secret door. And this one might really be their ticket out.

Day One
Administrated T to four leeches. Their single-minded biology makes them perfect candidates

*for this research, but they may be too simplistic
to adapt. No immediate changes observed.*

The word *four* was underlined. In the margin, someone had scrawled "change sequence" in a spidery hand, and circled it.

It was part of a lab journal, mostly dates and numbers. Rebecca had been about to set it back down when she'd seen that several phrases and words had been underlined on one of the last pages. She read on, looking for more of the marked passages.

*Day Eight
A week now. Rapid growth to double their former size, signs of transformation emerging. Spawning successful, their numbers doubled, but cannibalistic behavior has been initiated, presumably due to increase in appetite. Hastened to augment food supply, but lost two.*

Numbers doubled and *two* were underlined.

*Day 12
Provided them with live food but lost half when prey fought back. However, they are learning from experience, beginning to exhibit group attack behavior. Evolution is exceeding expectations.*

Lost half was underlined.

There were no more marked entries, but Rebecca skimmed on, disturbed by the success of the strange experiment.

Day 23, leeches no longer exhibit individual traits, can move as a collective. Day 31, breeding at a fantastic rate, eating everything offered now . . .

The last entry painted clearly for her just how far into madness Dr. Marcus had slipped.

Day 46
A day worthy of remembrance. Today, they began to mimic me. They recognize their father, I believe. I feel such strong affection for them, from them. Do they love? I think they do. It's us, now, only me and my brilliant children. No one will take them away from me.

With all that I've learned, they wouldn't dare.

"Hey!"

It was Billy, calling up through the floor. Rebecca set the papers down and walked to the hole, kneeling next to it.

"Did you find anything useful?" she asked, looking down at him.

"Maybe. Catch," he said, tossing something small up through the hole. Rebecca caught it. It was another of the leech keys, this one green.

"Is there a door up there with a bust of Marcus on the front?" Billy asked.

Rebecca shook her head. "I don't know. Not in this room, anyway. I've been reading more about his whacko experiments. Want me to go take a look around?"

Billy hesitated. "Why don't I come up, we can both look. Just let me find another table or something . . ."

"I'll be careful," Rebecca said. "Didn't you say there was another door down there? Maybe you should try and get it open while I see if I can find the keyhole for this thing."

"It's a combination lock," Billy said. "Unless you have a set of picks handy, I don't think we're going to get it open."

Rebecca sighed. Too bad Jill Valentine wasn't with them. She was on the Alpha team, and according to Barry, she could break into anything . . .

. . . *"change sequence."*

"Wait. Combination lock?"

Billy nodded, and Rebecca edged back from the hole, hurrying to the desk with Marcus's notes. She quickly read through the marked passages, did the math as she hurried back. *Four leeches . . . Doubled . . . Lost two . . . Lost half . . .*

"Try . . . four-eight-six-three," she said.

"Wild guess?" Billy asked.

Rebecca smiled faintly. "Probably. Just check." She held up the green leech carving. "I'll see if I can find where this goes."

Billy nodded, reluctantly, and Rebecca stood up, started for the room's door, not sure if she was being brave or stupid. She didn't really want to do anything alone, not since her encounter with the primates, but as long as she was already on the first floor, it made sense for her to take a look.

The lab's door opened into a short corridor, three doors besides the one she'd come through. The first door, on the right, was locked. The second door, around a corner and also to the right, was open, but a quick glance inside showed nothing but a large, empty room, a small office set to one side. It was too dark to see much else. Rebecca closed the door, relieved that she was already two-thirds of the way through her little search, and went to the last door, at the end of the corridor.

Also unlocked. Rebecca pushed it open, saw yet another door only a meter in front of her; to the left, the room opened up into what appeared to be the same lab she'd started from . . . It wasn't, but with the way the rooms were oriented, it had to be connected to the first lab. Maybe they'd split it up at some point—

—A movement. There, near a table by the connecting wall, was one of the infected, a gaunt, sallow man, his eyes blank, his mouth open and hungry. He shuffled toward her, making a soft gurgling sound in the back of his throat.

He was slow, very slow. Rebecca looked between him and the door in front of her, the weight of the leech-key warm in her hand. Taking a chance, she stepped forward and pushed at the door, was through and quickly closing it behind her before the too-thin zombie could take another step.

She'd stepped into an operating room, old and unclean, the once sterile tiles gray with a light film of scum, a few metal gurneys standing about on tilted wheels. And there, across from her and to the left, was a greenish door with a profile of Dr. Marcus on the front.

"Gotcha," she said, moving to the door, studiously avoiding a closer look at the operating table set in the room's far corner after she caught a glimpse of the heavy restraints attached. She had an idea of what Marcus had been up to; she didn't need to suffer the details.

The small leech fit perfectly into a depression just under the likeness of Dr. Marcus, and she heard the sound of a latch giving way. The door opened—

—and she took a step back, staggered by the smell, an odor she'd become all too familiar with.

The narrow room was lined on both sides with morgue drawers, several of them standing open. There were two bodies on the floor, neither moving, but she trained her handgun on the closest, all the same. Breathing shallowly, she walked inside.

God, please let there be something here worth locking up, she thought, stepping past an overturned gurney. *And let it be in plain sight, if it's not too much trouble.* There was no way she was going to search each drawer.

At the far end of the room was an offshoot to the right. Rebecca stepped over the second body, turned the corner, trying not to gag at the atrocious smell. There was another metal gurney pushed to one side—and on top was a single metal key.

She picked it up, feeling a mix of emotion. She'd found something, that was good—but whoopee, another key. It could go anywhere, could be the key to Marcus's summer home for all she knew.

Maybe that first door in the corridor . . .

"Rebecca?"

She pocketed the key and picked up her radio, moving toward the door as she answered.

"Yeah. What's up, over." She moved through the operating room, stopping at the door that led back to the partial lab. She'd want to run through to the corridor's entrance, avoid having to shoot that zombie if she could . . .

"There's no dial on the lock," Billy said, sounding irritated. "I went back and checked Marcus's office, but I didn't see anything. You had any luck, over?"

"Maybe," she said. "Let me check on one thing. I'll meet you back at the library, over."

"Careful. Over and out."

Careful. Rebecca shook her head slightly as she clipped the radio back to her belt, astounded at how fast a relationship could change, given the right—or wrong—circumstances. Only a few hours ago, she'd threatened to shoot him, had been convinced that he was ready to shoot *her*. Now, they were . . . Well, "friends" was probably not the right word, but it was seeming awfully unlikely that they'd end up killing one another.

For the first time in a while, she wondered what her teammates were doing. Was the manhunt for Billy still on? Had they been looking for her, for Edward? Or had they run into troubles of their own, been caught out by the fallout from the T-virus spill? . . .

. . . *and speaking of.* She listened at the door a moment, heard nothing. Taking a deep breath, she pushed the door open, quickly stepping across the short distance to the next door, not even looking into the lab. As she closed the door behind her, she heard a muffled wail of frustration, and felt a surge of pity for the hollow-eyed victim. The guy had probably worked here, but she wouldn't wish the zombie sickness on her worst enemy. It was a bad way to go, hands down.

She walked to the first door she'd tried, hoping the key would work, doubting that it would. She supposed they'd have to do a more thorough search for whatever it unlocked, or just keep looking for something else, another map, another key, another hole in a floor somewhere; it was disheartening, to say the least. If they couldn't turn anything up, they'd have to use the elevator again, take their chances above ground—

She slipped the key into the door's lock and turned it, heard and felt the lock give.

"No shit," she mumbled, grinning, and opened the door.

Something huge and dark leaped for her, howling.

Billy waited at the hole between the first and second floors, idly wondering if there was a way to blow that dial-lock door open with one of the Magnum shells—and heard a terrible, inhuman cry echoing down from the first floor, followed by one, two shots.

He didn't think to try the radio. He hopped onto the low table beneath the hole, hefted the shotgun through, then jumped after it, catching the edge with his hands. He'd doubted his abilities before, but now it didn't cross his mind that he might not be able to pull himself up. With a grunt of exertion, he lifted his body through the hole, first scrabbling to his elbows, then getting one knee up.

He grabbed the shotgun and was on his feet in time to hear that animal scream again, a strange and unearthly sound, like a bird being shredded to pieces. He spent a half second orienting himself, finding the door, and then he was running.

He crashed through the door into a hall—and there was Rebecca backed against the wall opposite, one sleeve of her shirt torn, her arm scored with four deep scratches, pointing her weapon at—

—*what the hell*—

—at a monster, an immense, reptilian monster. It was humanoid, hugely muscled, its pebbled skin a dark, noxious green. Its arms were so long that its clawed hands almost touched the floor. When it saw Billy it dropped its thick jaw and screeched again, the small eyes in its flat, sloping skull practically glowing with malevolence. A thin stream of dark blood flowed from its upper chest, one of Rebecca's shots, but it didn't seem to be overly affected by the wound.

Try this, Billy thought, bringing the shotgun up as Rebecca opened fire again. He blasted the creature full in the face, pumped the weapon and fired

again, not waiting to see what the first round had
done—

—and the thing's face was *gone,* splashed across
the wall and floor behind it, its heavy body toppling.
A frothing river of blood poured from the shreds of
its neck, from what little was left of its head—a bit
of jawbone, of teeth, tatters of dark flesh.

Billy didn't move for a few seconds, listening,
searching for another sound, another movement, but
there was nothing. He turned his attention to Rebecca, who was gripping her injured left shoulder
with her right hand. Blood seeped from beneath her
fingers.

"The pack on my belt," she said. "There's a bottle
of antiseptic wash in there, some bandages and
tape . . . It just clawed me. It didn't bite."

She looked pale, wincing as Billy cleaned her
wound and taped it, but she bore up well, taking the
pain rather than giving in to it. It was bad, probably
needed stitches, but it also could have been a lot
worse. When he was finishing up, she nodded toward
the half open door across from them.

"It was locked in there. The thing, I mean."

She sounded shocked, dazed. Billy walked to the
door, wanting to be in the way of anything else that
might come popping out. He stopped at the headless
monster, stood looking down at it.

"Kinda looks like the Creature from the Black

Lagoon on steroids," Billy said, glancing back, hoping for a smile. He got one, shaky but real, and once again, was impressed with her fortitude. It was rare, to be able to recover so quickly from an unexpected attack, especially by a nightmare like the monster in front of him. Most people would be shaking for hours afterward.

Rebecca moved to stand beside him. She nudged one of the creature's bulky legs with her boot. "Amazing," she said. "The things they were doing out here. Genetic engineering, recombinant viruses . . ."

"I think 'psychotic' is the word you're looking for," Billy said.

She nodded. "Can't argue that. Let's see if it was guarding anything important."

They stepped around the creature, Rebecca explaining what she'd found on the rest of the floor as they moved into the room. It was a kennel of some kind, but Billy was fairly certain it hadn't been used to board dogs; there were stacks of steel bar cages, many of them fitted with restraints, and the smell in the air was that of wild animals, a gamy, rank odor.

". . . which is where I found the key to this room," she was saying. "I was hoping that meant there'd be something useful here."

The room was u-shaped, split by shelves. They moved around the shelves, Rebecca letting out a small sound of disgust. Heaped in the far corner was a heap of torn fur and gnawed bones, what appeared to be the remains of a few of those baboon creatures. There was a lot of feces scattered about, too, dense piles of a black, tarry substance that smelled like—well, like shit. It seemed the monster had been locked up for a while.

There was a small wood table between two of the cage stacks, a few papers scattered across the top. Billy walked over—stepping carefully—and picked up the page on top as Rebecca started poking through a few of the open cages. It appeared to be part of a report.

. . . and yet research to date has shown that when the Progenitor virus is administered to living organisms, violent cellular changes cause breakdowns in every major system, most consistently the CNS. Furthermore, no satisfactory method has been found to control the organisms for use as weapons. Clearly, greater coordination at the cellular level is essential to enable further growth.

Experiments on insecta, amphibia, mammalia (primate) have all fallen short of projected results. It appears that no further progress can be made without using humans as the base or-

ganism. Our recommendation at this time is that the experimental animals be kept alive for further study and as possible prey for field testing of newer suggested hybrid B.O.W.s, such as the upcoming Tyrant series.

Jesus. Billy rifled through the pages, looking for the rest of the report, but there were only a handful of coffee-stained feeding schedules.

Tyrant series. All the creatures we've seen . . . And they were working on something that could conceivably kick said creatures' asses.

"Ha!"

Billy looked up, saw Rebecca holding something small up in the air, a triumphant grin on her face.

"Dial, anyone?"

He dropped the report back on the table. "You're kidding me."

"Nope. It was in one of the cages." She tossed the item to him. Billy caught it, felt his own grin surfacing. It was exactly what he'd been looking for, a rounded knob made to fit on the front of the combination lock downstairs.

"Four eight six three?" Billy asked, and Rebecca nodded.

"Four eight six three," she repeated, and held up her hand, showing him her crossed fingers. Billy crossed his own. It was dumb, a child's superstition, but he was long past the point of caring whether or not he appeared rational. Anything that could help, he'd give it a shot.

"Let's go see," he said, feeling hope resurface yet again as they moved out of the monster's room, amazed at how resilient that particular feeling was. There was a quote somewhere, about how as long as there was life, there was hope. He'd heard it when he'd been on trial, had thought it obvious and stupid at the time. How strange and somehow marvelous, that he would discover the truth of that statement fighting for his life in such very different circumstances.

Together, they headed back for the lab. Billy kept his fingers crossed.

†TWELVE

He watched the young twosome crawl down from the hole, make their way back to the combination door. Finally, they'd found a way to get it open; he'd expected them to break the lock, but one of them had apparently found the leech growth records, had worked out the code.

It seemed a single Hunter, a lone knight, was no match for them. The young man was surprised, but not overly so, watching as they opened the locked door. They possessed some small animal cleverness, these two; how sad for the world that they had to be destroyed.

The young man smiled. Humanity would surely recover from the loss, in ample time to effect Umbrella's crucifixion. Besides, the children were already in place.

Billy pushed the door to the cable car hanger open, the two of them smiling, congratulating one another as they "discovered" their means of escaping the lab. The cable car was operational, although they wouldn't be operating it; their lives were mere seconds from ending. The children watched from the shadows beneath the car, from the half-drained sewers, gathering into humanoid form, one, two of them. With a thought, a sigh, the young man released them from harness, sent the two bishops lurching towards their prey.

A sound, a scream. He frowned, turned one of the false men to see what had cried out from the darkness behind them—and it was attacked by an Eliminator, the primate jumping on the humanoid collective from out of nowhere, howling as it ripped into the midst of the children with dripping jaws.

From the platform, Rebecca and Billy were alerted by the sound of the fight, were ready with their weapons. Furious, torn, the young man hesitated, wanting to finish them, to kill, but concerned for the children—

He sent them forward, ignoring the primate's attack, letting the many stream away from its vicious jaws, reform again at the edge of the platform next to the second collective. The two false men clambered over the rail, eager to taste of the interlopers. The Eliminator followed, leaping after them.

He watched in horror as Billy got off a single blast at one of the false men with his shotgun, managing a clear shot. The young man felt the many screaming, felt the hive diminish, and his fury intensified, was fraught with anguish now, too, as Billy fired again, Rebecca joining in with her handgun. In bare seconds, one of the collectives was effectively destroyed.

"No, *no!*" The many had never faced a shotgun, he'd had no idea they could be so readily injured by it, but he couldn't retreat now, not in mid-attack. His racing thoughts told the survivors to rally, to join with the second false man as the Eliminator leaped for Billy, snatched at him with thick claws. The primate grappled with the killer—and then the two of them went over the rail, disappearing into the sewers with a mighty splash.

Rebecca screamed, rushed to the railing, but the second collective was almost upon her now. The young man felt a hot satisfaction, watching as the false man extended one magnificent arm, slapped at Rebecca's stupid, screaming face hard enough to knock her down. She rolled away as he paused, deciding how best to finish her. The loss to the hive was tremendous, unprecedented, he wanted to be sure she paid for it in full—

—except she was rolling to her feet now, holding

Billy's dropped shotgun, her face contorted with rage. She fired at the collective, blew one of its arms away, the children shrieking in pain as she fired again, and again.

The young man could barely see her now, the gazes upon her too few, many of the watchers dying even as he struggled to maintain contact. His last vision of her was a watery outline, a shadow growing darker, finally disappearing altogether.

Around him, the many wept, their salt tears blending into their joined tracks, the sorrowful smell of ocean rising up from their despairing mass. The young man closed his eyes, wept with them, but not for long. His anger was too great; she had to die, as her murdering boyfriend had surely died.

He didn't dare risk more of the children . . .

The Tyrant. His king.

He managed a smile. His anger was great; his wrath would be greater still.

There was a Magnum on the cable car, locked in the cold, rubbery fingers of a dead man. As the small aerial car made its short journey from one platform to another, gliding silently through the unknown dark, Rebecca pried the revolver free. It was unloaded. She remembered that Billy was carrying a couple of speed loaders with .50 caliber Magnum shells, but he was . . .

. . . is, *he* is *alive and I'm going to find him,* she told herself firmly, stepping from the cable car once it swung to a stop, ignoring the terrified voice in the back of her mind, the part that kept insisting he was surely dead. Billy was gone, lost to the fast-moving sewer beneath the cable car platforms, which had swept him and that monster in this direction, but he was alive, and she was going to find him. The thought cycled, repeated itself; she owed him that hope, that belief, several times over.

The second cable car platform was much like the first, small and cold and dark, but there was a set of stairs leading up and out of the hangar. Rebecca took a minute to resituate her weapons, to reload the nine-millimeter. Billy had the remaining shotgun shells on him, but he'd reloaded after that monster had attacked her outside the kennel room—

—after he saved your life, again—

—and there were still two rounds left; she wouldn't leave it behind, nor did she think it wise to leave the Magnum. She never knew when she might find another cache of ammo. The heavy revolver dragged on her belt, the shotgun hard on her injured shoulder, but she wanted to be ready for anything.

He's dead, Rebecca. You have to save—

No.

—save yourself now, have to—

No!

She hurried up the stairs, ignoring her body's fatigue, *have to find him, have to.* At the top of the flight, a door, the door opening into a massive, mostly empty warehouse room, the far end open to the night. Rebecca walked across the bare room, stepping over the floor's transport track, moved past rusting barrels that lined the walls, her mind too full of Billy for her to think straight. If he was hurt, if he was—

Dead. He might be dead. She started to reject the thought out of hand, but this mental voice wasn't terrified, wasn't in a blind panic; it was calm. Reasonable. She took a few deep breaths, stood a moment on the industrial platform elevator that bordered the big room, studied the cool, deep blue sky of early morning; the clouds were finally breaking up, a handful of pale, distant stars shining down. The storm had passed. She hoped it was an omen of good things to come . . . But she could only hope. If Billy was dead—and he probably was—she would have to deal with it.

But I'm not doing anything until I know.

There was a control console on the platform elevator's north side. Rebecca studied the controls a moment, finally deciding she should descend to the lowest level listed, B-4, try to find an entrance to the sewers there. She pushed the control button. The huge, octagonal platform jerked, then started down, the walls of the massive well that surrounded the platform sliding up and past, the night sky dwindling overhead.

The elevator finally settled into an expansive room, utilitarian, all gray walls and steel. To her right was a small office marked SECURITY, and a short hall that ended at another, more conventional elevator, like from an office building. To her left, a cave-in; mounds of rubble heaped up to a low, broken ceiling—and there appeared to be a second elevator there, in front of the stacked debris, this one bigger, a warehouse lift.

She stepped from the platform, checking for signs of life in the poorly lit room, her steps curiously quiet on the chipped concrete. It was empty. She moved to the security office, found it locked—but a glance through the grimy window set into the door told her there was nothing there worth scavenging.

She sighed, unsure which way to go. Her plan was to keep descending, her hope that eventually, she'd make it to water, but either elevator might lead her in the wrong direction.

So, pick one. It's better to be wrong than to waste time trying to decide. Right. She mentally flipped a coin, then headed for the elevator west of the platform.

She reached for the control panel, for the single button there—

—and a soft *ping* sounded, as the elevator came to a stop on her floor.

She scrambled back, there was no time, no place to run. She flattened herself in the corner as close to the doors as she could get, praying that whoever it was would be in too much of a hurry to look behind them.

The doors slid open. She held the shotgun ready, held her breath as a lone figure stepped out, a big man, wearing a vest—

Rebecca lowered the shotgun, eyes wide as Enrico Marini spun around, aiming his nine-millimeter at her.

"Don't shoot!"

She saw surprise, the shock of recognition register on his face, and then he pulled up, aimed at the ceiling.

"Rebecca," he said, relaxing slightly, and she noticed the dirt on his hands and face, the smears of blood on his arms. The knuckles of both hands looked battered and bruised; his S.T.A.R.S. vest was ripped in several places. Obviously, she hadn't been the only Bravo team member struggling to survive. "Are you okay?"

"You're alive," she said, stepping forward, so happy to see him that she didn't know how she wasn't crying with relief. He clumsily embraced her with one arm, patting her shoulder before stepping away.

"The others?" she asked.

Enrico turned, looked toward the industrial lift. "They came ahead. We were looking for Edward, and you."

She lowered her eyes. "Edward—he didn't make it."

Enrico's gaze hardened slightly, but he only nodded. "Did you see the rest of the team come through?"

"No."

"They must have just missed you," he said. "We found these documents . . ." He shook his head, as if denying a story that would take too long to tell. She understood completely.

"Due east of here is an old mansion," he continued. "We believe that Umbrella uses it for research. Come on. We can catch up to them if we hurry."

He started to walk away, and she felt her heart knot, a hot, hard fist in her chest.

"Wait!" she blurted, before she could think twice. "I've got to find Billy."

Enrico turned, stared. "Billy Coen? You found him?"

"Yes, but we got separated, and . . ." She trailed off, not sure how to explain.

"No point worrying about him," Enrico said. "He won't make it, anyway. Let's go."

"Sir, I—" She swallowed, forced herself to meet

his gaze. "It's a long story. But I—I need to find him. Don't worry, I'll catch up with you."

"Rebecca," he started, then seemed to read something in her voice, in her face, perhaps the same story she'd read in his—too much had happened, and any explanation would probably take longer than either of them could afford.

"Be careful," he said, and she drew herself up, gave him a firm nod, the acknowledgement of one professional to another. He turned and started away. She watched him go, watched as he reached the pile of rubble on the other side of the vast room, turned to the elevator there, disappeared from her sight.

I finally find my team, and tell them to go ahead without me, she thought, too weary to be astounded by her decision. They were alive, at least. As soon as she found Billy, she—*they*—would head east, catch up to the team at the Umbrella mansion.

She checked the elevator that Enrico had appeared from, found that it only went up. That made her decision easier, anyway. She walked across the room to the other one. She pushed the recall button, heard the creak and jerk of movement, the mechanism humming from somewhere inside the shaft. It was slow, crawling back from wherever Enrico had taken it. Rebecca leaned against the door, wishing it would hurry. She was too tired to stop moving, afraid that she might not get started again.

A large chunk of rock rolled down from the shadows at the top of the debris pile, hit the cement floor not far from where she stood, broke into several pieces. It was quickly followed by another, then a third—and then a small avalanche, many of the slabs shifting, resettling as a small cloud of dust rose up from the fallen debris. Rebecca stepped back from the elevator door, eyeing the pile nervously.

Crunch. Crunch. Crunch.

What sounded like heavy footsteps, coming from the mound of wreckage. More rock shifted, clattered to the floor.

"Enrico?" she asked, her voice hopeful and very small in the dust-choked air.

Crunch.

Crunch.

She pushed the recall button again. From the sound, the elevator continued to inch closer, but now she could see something moving, something in the shadows. Something big. And it was coming for her.

Billy held on to the broken remains of an eroded support pillar, waves and eddies of cold, dark water rushing past him, working to loosen his numb fingers. He held tight, half conscious, tried to assess, to resolve. He could barely think at all. He remembered the monkey—

—baboon, she said—

—attacking, its dirty claws sinking into his upper arms, remembered hitting the railing, hard. Remembered the splash of grimy water, the oily, sour taste and smell of it as it washed over him, Rebecca shouting his name, her voice fading as the current carried him away. There was the gurgling scream of the panicked animal as it let go, was drawn under—and then there was an outcropping of rock, and a sharp pain at one temple, and—and now he was here. Somewhere.

He was hurt, dizzy, lost. To his right, the waters gathered and roared, pushing their way through a giant pipe that led into darkness, a pipe more than big enough to swallow him whole. There was some kind of walkway perhaps ten meters to his left, suspended over the swirling water, but it might as well have been ten klicks, for his chances of getting to it. The water was too fast, too wild, and he wasn't the best swimmer even on a good day.

He held on. It was all he knew how to do.

Thirteen

The creature that pulled itself up and out of the rubble was like nothing Rebecca had ever seen before. It stood up near the top of the debris pile, raised its arms as though stretching, allowing her a clear look at it, making her mouth go dry, her palms sweat. She had a sudden, desperate urge to go to the bathroom.

It was humanoid. Human, almost, in that it had the facial features of a man—except no man glowed so pale, its hairless skin, its body, a luminous near-white. No man had claws that extended almost the length of his arms, the talons curved and shining like steel knives, longer on the right hand than on the left. The thick ropes of its veins were visible through its skin; masses of red and white tissue humped over its huge shoulders, across its massive chest. Clusters of blood-red sores were liberally scattered over its three-meter tall body, and much of its lower face had been ripped away, revealing a bleeding, flesh-and-bone grin, which it turned to Rebecca now, snicking its talons as though greatly anticipating their meeting.

The creature looked down at her, its impossible grin seeming to widen slightly. She could hear it breathing, a harsh rasping sound, could actually see the pump of its strange, pulsing heart, only partly shielded by its ribcage.

Barely aware that she'd raised the shotgun, Rebecca fired.

The blast peppered its chest with black, sudden ribbons of blood sliding down its body, and it threw back its huge, bald head and screamed, a sound like Armageddon, like the end of everything. There was more rage, more fury than pain, and Rebecca suddenly understood that she wasn't going to survive very much longer.

With a single, graceful leap, the monster sprang from the pile of shattered rock, hit the floor not four meters away in a crouch. Rebecca could feel the ground tremble. Its steel talons raked against the concrete as it drew itself up, its gray, malignant gaze fixing on her. She backed away, pumping the shotgun, her entire body shaking as she tried to aim, tried to target its horrible grin. It stepped closer, came between her and the elevator—just as she heard the elevator car slide to a stop, heard the door unlatch.

The creature took another step. *At least it's slow; if I can lure it away, then run back—*

Another step, and she could hear and see a crack appear in the pavement beneath its thick black toenails. She moved back, tried to lengthen the distance between them—

—and suddenly it was running, *fast,* a blur as it dropped one arm, sweeping it up, the blades of its hands close enough for her to see a reflection of her own movement as she dove out of the way. She did a shoulder roll, clutching the shotgun to her chest, coming to her feet even as the creature finished its strange, sweeping run. Sparks flew up from the wall next to the elevator, a control panel ripped apart—

—and behind her, lights flashed, an alarm sounded—and a massive metal door between her and the platform elevator she'd come down on began to close, sliding down. It would cut the room in half—and trap her with the freakish monster.

She ran, determined to be on the other side of that door. It was heavy and dropping fast, a thick slab of metal—surely impenetrable to the creature.

She cleared it easily, turned to watch, running backward.

The manmade monstrosity started after her, ducking beneath the lowering panel. She felt her heart hammering, a sheen of sweat breaking out across her body; if she ended up on the same side as that thing, it was all over.

She waited, the creature moving toward her slowly, surely—and as the bottom of the door reached the level of her head, she ran back to the other side, having to duck herself, praying that the thing would end up trapped.

It started to follow again, crouching, raising its claws over its head as it moved under the door. She felt a flash of hope, that the door would crush it—and then she heard metal screech as its giant talons dug grooves into the lowering panel. She watched in horror, in amazement, as it actually slowed the door's descent just enough for it to get underneath. Then it was through, and the door settled to the floor with a resounding *clang*.

Her every instinct was telling her to run, to get away—but there was nowhere to go. With that door coming down, the room was barely bigger than her studio apartment. She had to get inside that elevator. It was her only chance.

She broke for it, grabbed the handle to the door, started to slide it open—and heard the monster coming, heard the pound of its heavy feet, the crack of cement as it thundered toward her.

Shit! She didn't even turn, instinctively knowing that there wasn't time. She dropped instead, fell to her knees and scrambled to one side—just as those claws came crashing down, hacking into the elevator door, piercing the wall where she'd been standing only a second before.

She stumbled backward as the monster turned, fixed its gaze on her again, took a step. It was as focused, as relentless as some kind of machine. It drew one overlong arm back, like it was going to toss a ball, perhaps, and took a second rumbling step.

Think, think! She couldn't outfight it, probably couldn't kill it with what she had left; her only hope was to trick it somehow . . .

The plan was still forming even as she put it into action. The creature was too big, it couldn't easily stop once it started to run; if she got it moving, ducked out at the last second, she might have time to get the elevator door open. She stopped moving, as far from the elevator as she could get in the small space.

Another step. The talons snicked. It took all of her will not to break and run. She kept the shotgun pointed at the creature, readied herself to dive for the elevator as soon as it picked up speed.

The monster's grin widened as its knees bent slightly, as it readied to spring—

—and then it was moving, only a few running steps and it would be on her. Rebecca flew, ducked and ran, slamming into the elevator door, grabbing at it with trembling, hurried hands. She jerked the door open, blundered inside, turned to close the door—

—and the thing was already fixed on her again, already moving fast, much too fast. The door wouldn't hold, she knew it. She brought the shotgun up, no time to aim, fired.

The blast caught its right shoulder. It staggered back, screaming, blood flying from its shredded wound, and then Rebecca saw nothing more. She slammed the door closed, hit the lowest button on the board, squeezed her eyes shut and started to pray.

Seconds passed. The elevator continued down, down—and finally came to a stop. She stopped praying long enough to hear the rushing water outside—*must be the sewer*—but she was too freaked to care much for the moment, her body still trembling wildly.

After what seemed a long time, the shaking subsided. She was okay . . . or alive, at least, and that was something. With a final prayer that she might never see that thing again, Rebecca pushed the door open and stepped out.

* * *

William Birkin was finally—finally!—leaving when he heard the inhuman scream echo through the otherwise silent facility, a scream of pure rage. He stopped at the entrance to the small, underground tunnel that led to the outside, looking back toward the executive control room. He'd spent the last two hours in the tiny, hidden area, first struggling to make the decision, then struggling to make the computer obey his override commands. The destruct sequence was set for just over an hour; as Wesker had suggested, the obliteration of the facility and its surrounding complex would coincide with the beginning of a new day.

That scream . . . He'd never heard anything like it, but knew immediately what it was, having seen the project in its final stages. Nothing else could make such a sound. The Tyrant prototype was loose.

The shadows that bordered the narrow tunnel suddenly seemed too deep, too lonely. Too capable of secrecy. Birkin turned and hurried away, sure now that he'd made the right decision.

It was all going to burn.

Billy heard something. He lifted his heavy head, managed to turn it slightly. There, to his left, a door opened onto the walkway, and out stepped a human figure.

"Hey," he called, but he couldn't manage any volume, the sound of his voice lost to the rushing water. He closed his eyes.

"Billy!"

He looked again, felt warmth welling up deep inside. Rebecca, it was Rebecca leaning over the railing, calling his name, and the sight and sound of her brought him around some, pushed the bone-weary exhaustion away, just a little.

"Rebecca," he said, raising his voice, not sure if she could hear. He tried to think of something to tell her, some action she should take, but could only say her name again; the situation was self-explanatory, and he was in a bad way. If she wanted to help him, she'd have to come up with something on her own.

"Billy, look out!" Rebecca was gesturing wildly with one hand, fumbling for her handgun with the other.

The terror in her voice woke him up. He clutched the support pillar tighter, tried to pull himself up, to see what she was pointing at—and caught just a glimpse of something moving fast, something long and dark slipping through the water like a giant serpent, rushing at him.

He tried to move, to edge around the pillar, but the water was too fast, he couldn't let go. He'd be lost in less than a second.

Rebecca fired, once, twice—and the unseen creature slammed into the support pillar hard enough to shake him free.

He yelled, paddling furiously to stay above the frothing water, to resist the pull of the emptying pipe, but it was no good. In seconds, he was swept into the dark, pushed and pummeled, the sound of the water filling his ears as it carried him away.

Fourteen

In the midst of Rebecca's brief battle with the proto-Tyrant, William Birkin sneaked out of the facility, his head low, his proverbial tail tucked between his legs. The young man had lost track of him a few hours earlier, had assumed that the scientist had followed Wesker up and out—those people from Rebecca's little adventure team had, only moments before—but there he was, half running through one of the hidden exit tunnels, his pallid, twitching face a mask of fear. Terrified by the sounds of the battle, certainly, entirely unaware that he was alive only because his life was so very unimportant.

Although he'd wished to deal with him personally, the young man let the scientist go now, prey for another day. He was too enraptured by the fight, too eager to see Rebecca torn limb from limb. Instead, he saw her duck her fate yet again, a combination of deftness and stupid luck that was quite a marvel to behold. He watched as she left the Tyrant behind and came across Billy only a moment later, somehow still alive, clinging like a barnacle to a rock as a sea of sewer water churned around him. A single blow by one of the water creatures sent him spiraling away to one of the plant's many filter rooms, left Rebecca screaming after him, surely half mad with frustration, with loss and crushed hope.

The young man smiled, a cold and nasty smile, calmer than he'd felt for some time as he watched Rebecca cross the walkway, find another elevator in the plant's operations room, wend her way toward the depths of the plant—where he and his hive waited, curling together in their cocoon of glittering liquid excretions. With luck, she'd come across Billy soon, possibly even alive. Probably, in fact. He understood now, that he'd simply tried too hard to rush matters, to hurry their fate. A confrontation was inevitable . . . And hadn't he truly wanted an audience all along, someone to appreciate his magnificent undertaking? Besides, the dawn would be soon, a dangerous time for the children, their delicate bodies easily burned by even the weakest sunlight; better that he let the two interlopers come to him. They would know his glory before he crushed them himself.

He watched and waited, excited for the final chapter of his triumph to begin.

Rebecca wasn't sure where she was, the descending levels and rooms of the new building impossibly tangled, but she kept going, kept moving down. The hallways were clear, but two of the rooms she moved through—yet another small control room of unknown purpose, and a wrecked employee lounge—were infested with zombies. She only had to shoot two of seven that she saw, the rest too decrepit, too slow-moving to constitute a real threat. She wished she had the time and the ammo to put all of them down, to spare them what their lives had become, but seeing Billy again kept her hurrying. He was hurt but alive, and hidden somewhere in the depths of the confusing layout.

The new facility was a water treatment plant, she could tell that from the pervasive odor, if not from the signs and control boards that seemed to litter every other room, but she thought that it was also a front for more of Umbrella's illegal activities; why else would it be connected to the training facility, albeit indirectly? She went through a small courtyard area on the seventh basement level—at least, she *thought* it was the seventh—that had been under construction before the virus had hit, and she doubted very much that the rock-carved bunker—replete with forklift—had much to do with water treatment.

Yeah, but what the hell do I know, she thought randomly, pushing herself to move faster, through another door, a room with a sunken pit full of crates to one side. Until tonight, she hadn't believed in zombies, or bio-weapon conspiracies . . . Truth be told, she hadn't really believed that such deliberate evil could exist. What she'd seen, what she'd experienced since stepping onto that train all those hours ago . . . Everything was different, now. She didn't know that she'd ever again be able to turn such a naive eye to the world around her, that she'd ever be able to look at a person or place without wondering what hidden face lay behind what she saw. She wasn't sure if she should be angry or grateful for the loss of innocence; if she stayed with the S.T.A.R.S., it would undoubtedly serve her well.

At the back of the room with the crates, a metal staircase. Rebecca stopped at the top, caught her breath as she looked down, grimacing with distaste, unsure of how to proceed. There were leeches on the stairs, at least a few dozen scattered across the steps, hanging from threads of slime or tracking glistening paths across the gray metal. She didn't want to get near them, afraid that they might attack if she got too close, or hurt one of them—but she didn't want to backtrack, either. She felt like time was speeding up, like things were happening fast and faster, that she had to keep up or risk being lost.

Or risk running into that thing again. That clawed killing machine. Its angry scream still echoed in her mind. She'd wounded it, but the chances that it had crawled away in some dark corner to die were slim to none. Things like that were never so accommodating.

Gritting her teeth, she carefully stepped over and around the leeches, pausing after each step, swallowing bile as one slid over the toe of her boot before continuing on its way. It was a short flight, at least; she got down without stepping on any of the horrid little things, reaching the door at the bottom without further incident.

When she opened the door, a cool mist sprayed across her sweating skin, the roar of emptying pipes like music. It was a big room, dominated by huge, jutting conduits to one side, water from them splashing down and over a series of mesh filters—

—and there, amid a scatter of random flotsam—

"Billy!"

Rebecca ran to Billy's prone form, a bitter waterfall splashing down beside them as she crouched, reached for his throat. She pushed his dog tags aside, shaking inside . . . But there was a strong, even pulse—and at her touch, he opened his eyes, looked blearily up at her.

"Rebecca?" He coughed, started to sit up, and she gently placed one hand on his chest, pushing him down. He had a purpling knot on his left temple, a big one.

"Just rest a minute," she said, having to force the words around the hardness in her throat. She'd wanted to believe he'd be all right, but it had been so hard . . . "Let me check you out."

A faint smile played across his lips. " 'Kay, but then it's my turn," he mumbled, and coughed again.

He answered her questions without any confusion as she pushed and prodded, checked his range of motion, cleaned a few of his deeper scratches. The knot on his head seemed to be the worst of his injuries, causing him some dizziness and nausea, but it wasn't nearly as bad as she'd feared—and after only a few minutes of her ministrations, he pushed himself into a sit, turning a weak smile her way.

"Okay, okay," he said, wincing as she touched his temple. "I'll survive, but not if you keep poking me."

"Right," she said, sitting back on her heels, feeling a surprisingly deep satisfaction; she'd set out to find him, and had. She'd had no idea that such a basic sense of accomplishment could be so fulfilling, could so easily overwhelm all of the negatives in their situation, even if only for a moment. "I'm glad you're alive, Billy."

He nodded, wincing again at the movement. "You and me both."

She helped him to his feet, supporting him as he found his balance. When he was steady enough, he stepped away—and she saw a look of disgust cross his face, his mouth curving down as he moved past her, toward one corner of the room where a slick of dark water poured over another mesh filter.

The corner of the room was heaped with bones. Human bones, worn smooth by years of falling water, thick with a greenish bacterial slime. Rebecca counted at least eleven skulls among the tumble of femurs and cracked ribs, most of them crushed or broken.

"Some of Marcus's old experiments?" Billy's tone was low; it wasn't really a question, and Rebecca didn't answer it, only nodding.

"It's Umbrella," she added, after a moment. "They encouraged it. They were all in it together."

Now Billy didn't answer, only stared at the bones, some unknown emotion in his dark gaze. After a second, he shook it off, turned away from the sad remnants of human life.

"What say we blow this Popsicle stand?" he asked, and though his words were light, neither of them smiled.

"Yeah," she said, reaching out to grab his hand for a moment, just a moment, squeezing his fingers tightly in her own. He squeezed back. "Yeah, that sounds good."

Billy felt like shit, but he soldiered on as Rebecca led them vaguely eastward, wanting more than anything to get free of Marcus's damned playground before he allowed himself to collapse. As they wandered through a maze of corridors and rooms—Billy was hopelessly lost after their second turn—she told him what had happened to her since he'd been dragged off the cable car platform. She'd had a run-in with her team leader, and a fight with some super-creature Frankenstein that she very nearly didn't survive. She'd also found a .50 Magnum revolver to match the ammo he'd been lugging around, some serious fire-power, and had managed to hang on to the shotgun. In all, he thought she'd done better than he probably would have, in the same circumstances.

They found an empty bunkroom and loaded up, Billy taking the Magnum, Rebecca keeping the shot-gun. There was a sealed gallon jug of water under one of the bunks and they took turns gulping it down, both of them desperate for hydration. It turned out that swimming in sewer water didn't do much for one's thirst.

Refreshed by the water, holding decent and fully

loaded weapons, Billy finally felt like he might recover from his ride through the rapids. They took the southern exit from the bunkroom, through an industrial treatment room, then another. The rooms of the plant blurred together for Billy, all looked the same—rusting metal walls and floors, pipe railings, huge walls of unknown equipment covered with dials and switches. Some of the equipment was working, filling the large rooms with echoing blasts of mechanical sound, though God only knew what it was controlling. Billy found that he didn't much care, though as they continued on, they could both hear the rush of water getting closer, *big* water—and when they went through a massive pump room that opened out into the chill of predawn, they found a walkway that spanned an actual dam.

They stood for a moment, looking out over the dark length of reservoir that ran alongside the building they'd emerged from, the crashing curtain of water that punctuated it at the far end. It was too loud for them to talk, and they stepped back into the pump room, both of them smiling. They'd found a way out, at least; true, the walkway over the dam led to another building, but just seeing the fading stars, the sinking moon, gave Billy a real boost. Their nightmare run through the Umbrella complex would be over soon, he could feel it, the end in sight as surely as the new day would soon dawn.

"My team probably went this way, cleared us a path," Rebecca said, looking hopeful. She had to speak up to be heard over the cascade of water just outside, the surging pumps that took up half of the room. Her voice rang slightly against the metal walk that surrounded a pool of water in the room's center. "He said they were going east. We're practically out of here already."

"I thought you said Enrico took that elevator up," Billy said.

"Oh, right," she said, her expression sagging. She blinked, and he realized how very tired she had to be. "Sorry. Forgot."

"Understandable," Billy said. "But you're right, we *are* practically out of here." He touched the Magnum on his belt, the loose handcuff on his wrist banging into it, a sudden reminder of his life before the jeep accident. That life seemed so far away now, like it had happened to a different man . . . But it was still waiting for him, somewhere outside.

Thoughts for later, for *if*. He managed a smile, patted the Magnum. "This is kind of a universal key—unlocks doors, clears out unwanted disease carriers, you name it."

Rebecca smiled back, started to say something— and stopped, staring into his eyes, both of them frozen at the sound of water splashing across the metal walk. As one, they turned to look—to see a giant rising up from the pool a few meters away, a thing that Billy knew instantly was the monster she'd told him about, from the elevator. It was huge, white, covered with blood and sores; it reached out to pull itself from the pool with insanely long, knifelike claws, the tips screeching against the walk.

Billy grabbed the Magnum, backing away, trying to push Rebecca behind him. She easily evaded his grasp, standing her ground with the shotgun, and Billy's heroic ideals dropped away when the creature saw them and let out a terrible scream, a deep, mind-ripping sound of hatred, of lust not just to kill, but to rend and mutilate. Facing it alone wasn't macho; it was suicidally stupid.

"When it gets moving, it doesn't maneuver well," Rebecca said quickly, half under her breath. He had to strain to hear her over the rhythmic beat of the powerful pump engines. "If we can get it away from the door, get it running, we can get past it when it tries to turn."

Billy took careful aim at the thing's rough-hewn face. It took a step toward them, and they both backed away. "How about we kill it instead?"

"Don't," Rebecca said, her voice edged with panic. "You'll just make it mad. What you're seeing now is after two shotgun blasts, one of them almost point blank."

The thing took another step and lowered itself

slightly, tensing its legs as though about to spring.

"Run!"

Billy didn't need to hear it twice. They both turned and ran, pivoted left where the walk did. Behind them, two, three massive, ringing steps sounded against the protesting metal—and then the monster's claws ripped down and across the wall at the corner, a tremendous shriek of sound as the thick steel curled up like wood shavings.

Billy turned, raised the Magnum as the stopped monster slowly turned to face them.

"Keep going!" he shouted to Rebecca, aiming for the pulsing red tumor half buried in its chest, what had to be its heart. The monster took a single step, its opaque gray eyes fixing on Billy, its claws raising.

Billy fired, the weapon jumping in his hand, roaring, deafening. A hole erupted in the thing's breast bone, not a direct hit to the heart but close. Blood poured from the hole, ran down its thick white gut. It howled, the sound even louder than the blast from the hand-cannon, and infinitely more deadly, but it didn't go down.

Jesus, that shoulda stopped an elephant—

"Come *on!*" Rebecca shouted, pulling at his arm. He shook her off, took aim again. If it bled, it could die, and short of a grenade launcher, the .50 Magnum was maybe the best weapon for the job.

The monster took a staggering step forward then

seemed to find its balance, its dead gaze focusing on Billy. Blood continued to pour from its wound, had drenched its sexless crotch now, the tops of its muscle-bound thighs. That grin, that horrible grin—it seemed to be laughing, as though it couldn't wait to share some private joke with him.

Billy thought the punchline probably included ripping an arm off and beating him to death with it. He fixed on the heart, squeezed the trigger—

—and another tremendous *bang*, more blood flying, the monster screaming—

—*oh, God, please let that be pain!*

—but not falling. Still, not falling. It was hard to tell where he'd hit it, there was blood everywhere, but the heart continued to pulse.

"Move!"

Billy was shoved aside, Rebecca stepping forward, raising the shotgun as the creature started to crouch, its legs tensing. She aimed, low, too low, there was no way she was going to hit its heart—

—and the shotgun boomed, and finally, the monster went down, its cry one of rabid fury. It clawed at the walk, its talons pulling a tremendously painful, high squeal from the metal.

Billy saw that Rebecca had blown out one of its knees, and hesitated only a second, just long enough to wonder why he hadn't thought of that. It wasn't dead, but unless it sprouted wings, it wasn't going to be coming after them anytime soon. Then he raised the Magnum again, fixing on its fish-belly white skull as it floundered and clawed to pull itself closer, undoubtedly to continue its attack. It only managed to slide itself partway into the water, the dark pool churning with pink foam as it struggled to get out.

"Waste of ammo," he half asked, glancing at Rebecca for her approval. As terrible as the thing was, he wouldn't feel right about letting it bleed to death, to suffer any more. It was another of Umbrella's victims, in a way; it hadn't asked to be born.

"Yeah," she said, nodding—but he could see the pity in her expression, could see that she felt the same way. "Do it."

Two rounds, the second just to be sure, and the massive body slipped soundlessly into the pool of water, disappearing beneath the surface.

Fifteen

They walked over the dam in the rising light, the deep blue of the early hours giving way to a soft, faded gray that hid all but the brightest stars.

Rebecca walked quietly alongside Billy, noticed that the clouds were clearing out. It would be another hot summer day, though at the moment, she was doing her best not to shiver; the sun wouldn't be up properly for another half hour, at least. She was tired, more than she could ever remember being, but just knowing that the long, horrible night was finally at its end, that a new day was here, was enough to keep her from flagging.

At the end of the dam walk was a short ladder leading to a door. The went up, Billy first, and stepped into a turbine room, more rusty metal railings around cement walks and heavy piped equipment lining the walls. There were two doors. The north door dead-ended in a storage room. The door to the west was standing open, led through a long, fenced corridor to another door.

"Keep going?" Billy asked, and Rebecca nodded. It was probably another dead end, but she wanted to keep from having to go back the way they'd come for as long as possible. They'd witnessed enough death and destruction already; she didn't want to have to go back for seconds.

She paused as Billy started down the walk, noticing a silvered edge to the heavy door. It was reinforced with steel, and there was a keycard reader next to it. Someone had wedged a stick under the bottom of the door to keep it open.

A wet stick, she thought, reaching down to touch the glistening wood. When she pulled her hand away, slender strings of goo clung to her fingertips, stretching away from the stick.

For a half second, she had a confused idea that for some reason, the leeches had propped the door open—then shook it off, reminding herself that there were leeches all over the facility. She wiped her hand on her vest and caught up to Billy, who was almost at the far end of the walk already, reloading the Magnum.

The door was unlocked, and Billy pushed it open. Another cement and metal entryway, leading down another short hall. Billy stepped inside, sighing, Rebecca sighing along with him. Would this place never end?

The room smelled like a beach at low tide, though they couldn't see anything from the entry, the room opening up just out of sight. They'd taken two steps inside when they heard the *click* of a lock, the door sealing behind them.

"Automatic lock?" Rebecca asked, frowning.

Billy stepped back to the door, rattled the handle. "It was closed before. Doesn't make sense that it would lock after we came through—"

Rebecca heard something then, a low sound that made her heart skip. The sound quickly rose, became a deep, cackling laugh from the room beyond the entryway.

Without a word, she and Billy walked away from the door, both of them holding their weapons tightly, stepped around the corner—

—and froze, staring at the vast sea of life that surrounded them, that seemed to cover every square inch of wall, that dripped and crawled across the ceiling, the floor. Leeches, thousands of them, hundreds of thousands. The room was a large one, high and wide, split by a small corridor that ran along the back wall. Incinerators lined a central construct that rose to the ceiling, openings in the metal showing flickers of fire. There was a big metal door on the south wall, set back into a recessed doorway, which appeared to be the only other way out—if they wanted to run through all those leeches, which Rebecca most definitely did not. The cavernous space was bi-level, a catwalk encircling the central construct, an open fire at one side of the upper walk casting a flickering glow over the black, bubbling sea that washed across the room's every nook and corner—and on the walk, a lone figure, a tall, broad-shouldered young man, laughing, his strong, strange voice carrying in the salt-scented, rotten air.

"Welcome," he said, and laughed again, a leech curled on each shoulder, others trailing down his extended arm. He was surrounded by the creatures. "So glad you could join us. You're the guests of honor . . . After all, this is your wake."

Rebecca only stared, stunned into silence, but Billy took a step forward, raising his voice.

"You're his son, aren't you? Or his grandson?"

Rebecca knew immediately who he was talking about, and found herself nodding. *Of course* . . .

"That's right," the young man said, smiling widely, a fiendish smile. "In a way, I'm both."

He made a shrugging motion with his arms—and changed, the transformation rippling over his body like water, like a movie effect. His long, dark hair shortened, turned white. His youthful features melted into aged ones, lines and creases forming, his eyes changing color, the pupils enlarging. In seconds, he was no longer the young man, though his smile was just as cold, just as brutal.

It was Billy's turn to be silent, as Rebecca breathed out the name, unable to believe that it wasn't another trick, another false face. "Dr. Marcus?"

The man on the catwalk nodded, and began to speak.

"Ten years ago, Spencer had me assassinated," he said, the memories flashing through his hive mind, the children remembering for him. The images were blurred and dark, indistinct in shape and color, but the feelings were as clear as they had been on the day he'd lost his life.

He had been expecting an attack for some time, but it had still come as a surprise. He'd been working in his lab, the children playing in the pool at his feet, when the door burst open—and then there was gunfire, loud and final. He remembered the pain as he fell to his knees, clutching at the holes in his chest, his gut—and remembered seeing two familiar faces, the men walking into the room, his brilliant disciples, his best students watching as he gasped his last breaths. Albert Wesker and William Birkin, both smiling, *smiling!*

He remembered the sense of loss, the incredible anger that clawed to the surface of his dying mind as his body fell, splashing into the pool, the children scattering as everything went to black . . .

. . . and then the memories changed, became the thoughts of the many. He could see his own face and body, half submerged, pale and ugly in death, but loved, so very loved by the hive mind. He had been their God, their creator and teacher, their father. They swam to him, wormed between his sagging lips, wiggled and strained to enter the gaping holes that had been blown through his poor flesh.

Marcus found his voice, telling the two stunned watchers what they needed to know, to understand. "They left me to rot, took my notes and closed my lab, leaving it all to the ruin of time. They didn't understand, you see. Time was what was needed. It took years for the T-virus inside my queen to reconstruct, to evolve . . . And to become the variation that created what I am now."

He smiled, relishing their mute awe, enjoying his moment in the sun of their wonder. "So, you are correct. I am Marcus, but I'm also Marcus's son, and grandson—and every other extension, all other offspring, the union between Marcus and his queen. *My* queen. She lives inside of me. She sings to her children."

At the intensity of his joy, his triumph, the children surged toward him, swam up his legs, tickled their way across his most familiar form, that of James Marcus. He reveled in the feeling, laughing aloud at the revulsion that crossed the faces of his two young guests. If only they knew! The phenomenal rapture he felt as part of the hive, its leader and follower—Marcus's death had freed him, had made him far greater than his human life ever would have allowed.

"I scattered the virus," he said. "The world will know, now, what Umbrella has done. What Spencer and his stupid greed have contrived. Umbrella will burn, but Marcus will be hailed as a god for what he created. I am the archetype of a new man, far superior to the lonely pattern of humanity; the world will seek me out, will beg to join the hive, to unite as one mind, one all-powerful being!"

The man, Billy, spoke again, his face curled in loathing, his voice tight with it. "You're dreaming. You're a sick, twisted freak, whatever you are—and the world *will* seek you out, but only to kill you, to put an end to your insane delusions!"

Such a fool, so self-righteous in his own stupidity! A great anger rose in him, in the children, tainting his joy. He could feel his body quake with it. "We'll see who's going to die," he said, his voice trembling with anger—

—but it was no longer Marcus's voice, he had become the young man again, the children's vision of Marcus as a youth. He frowned, not sure why he had changed, or how—he had not wished it, had not sung or willed the shift in form.

The children swept through him, swollen with his anger, ignoring his inner commands, and for the first time since he'd crawled from the pool only a few months ago, since the hive had given him his new life, he had no control over it. The many would not listen, wanted only to smite the intruders, to squash them.

The young man felt them rising to his throat, spilling out like bile, choking him. He tried to hold on, to exert his influence, but the anger was too big, too all-encompassing. He was changing, becoming something entirely new, and his struggle for domination was washed aside, lost to this new thing.

The queen! He could feel her consciousness filling him, her creative power surging forth, carried by the children to every part of his metamorphosing form. She wanted to kill, to destroy the two humans who dared to judge her, and she was far stronger than even he had imagined.

The thing that had once been Marcus had no choice but to surrender, to become the most powerful player of all. To become the queen.

Marcus started to change once more, in a way that seemed to surprise him as much as it surprised Billy.

Leeches began to pour from his mouth, gagging him, dozens of them sliding out in a rush of slime, hitting the floor like fat raindrops. The young man's eyes were wide, his expression one of disbelief as he continued to choke out the slick fall of leeches.

As soon as they hit the floor, the creatures rushed back to the young man, swarming up his body, attaching themselves, burrowing into him. Round shapes moved beneath his skin, tunneling, changing the shape and texture of his flesh. His clothes melted away as the leeches continued to swarm, giving his body a strangely rubbery appearance, his arms and legs starting to look like great masses of fat worms twined together. His face elongated, stretching, the skin tearing to expose ribbed striations of purplish muscle tissue, throbbing, turning thick and wet with goo.

Next to him, Rebecca drew a sharp breath as the Marcus-creature lost its human appearance entirely, its whole body made up of those fat worms now, stuck together by dripping webs of clear slime. It grew in size as well, the leeches near it joining the multitude, adding mass and height. Long, stringy tentacles shot up from its back, whipping around like streamers in a high wind, the color of inflammation, of infection.

"The queen," Rebecca breathed. "She's taking control."

Billy pointed the Magnum at the growing creature—

—and the thing flew upward, leaping straight into the air. It hit the ceiling with a huge, wet smacking sound and clung there a moment, dribbling thick fluids to the floor far below. Except for having four limbs, it no longer looked remotely human.

Billy fired at the ceiling but it was already gone, dropping to the floor in front of them, condensing slightly as it hit the ground like some giant rubber toy. It—*she*—stretched out again, towering over him and Rebecca, those dark tentacles snapping around toward them, reaching for them.

He and Rebecca both stumbled back. Billy felt his boots sliding as he stepped on any number of the leeches that still covered the floor, heard the soft, fat *pop* of each creature beneath his heels. Rebecca grabbed his arm, almost falling as she, too, slipped across the blanket of leech bodies.

The deaths of her ghastly children had an immediate effect. The leech queen pulled her tentacles back and let out a scream, a strange, high, warbling wail like nothing on earth, a sound made all the more horrible by its complete alienness. All of the leeches in the room started toward her at once, moving away from Rebecca and Billy, clearing a path from beneath and behind their killing footsteps.

The leech queen continued to grow as the small

bodies packed on, joining together with the core creature, her size almost doubled in less than a minute. Billy shot a look over his shoulder, saw that they were going to dead-end back at the door they entered by if they let the monster choose their path, in the most literal sense of the word.

At the room's south side was a closed door set into a kind of recessed entryway. There was a sea of leeches separating them from it, but the sea was on the move, flowing toward the growing Marcus-queen monster. She seemed oblivious to their presence as she packed on more of her hive, swelling to gargantuan size in a soft, sloshing whisper of liquid movement.

"South door," Billy said, keeping his voice low as they continued to slowly back away. They had to act now, fast, or their chance would be gone.

"If it's locked?" Rebecca whispered back.

"Gotta risk it," he said. "I'll cover. On three. One . . . two . . . *three!*"

Rebecca broke and ran as Billy opened fire, pouring rounds into the giant, bloated body of the queen. She screamed, her high wail taking on depths of pain, of hate, and shot a handful of tentacles at him, the appendages moving lightning quick.

They grabbed him, lifted him into the air. Billy lost the Magnum, couldn't get to his handgun as he was wildly shaken, his head snapping back and forth, his arms pinned by the creature's brute strength. Her tentacles curled around his chest, tightening like a vise, squeezing so hard that he couldn't draw breath. After only a few seconds, he could feel himself blacking out, the shaking world fading to brilliant spots of darting black.

He heard the sound of the shotgun—and the monster was screaming again, dropping him, spinning around to face her new attacker. Billy crashed to the floor. He ignored the pain, scrambled for the Magnum as a hundred leeches crawled toward him, as Rebecca fired again and the monster started for her, tentacles lashing all around.

Billy got to his feet, saw that Rebecca had her back turned. The second blast hadn't been aimed at the monster at all, but at a standing control console next to the south door. She fired again, kicking at the door at the same time. It flew open, but the queen was almost upon her, easily twice her height, heavier by far, *she'll rip her apart like a paper doll—*

"Hey!" Billy screamed, no time to reload the Magnum, had to get her attention fast—

—and he leaped into the nearest wave of leech bodies, jumping up and down, kicking and stomping as hard as he could. They burst by the dozen, spilled ichorous blood and goop across the floor, drenching his boots. He danced on their dying bodies, feeling a fierce, uninhibited satisfaction as the leech queen spun again, howling in distress.

He saw Rebecca make it through the door, had a half second to be glad about it—and then the monster was snatching him up again, throwing him across the giant room in a blind rage.

Billy slammed into the back wall. He felt a rib crack, then he was falling, landing heavily on the cement floor. It drove the wind out of him, but he was on his feet again in a second, running for the south door, leeches popping underfoot as he struggled to breathe.

The monster was about the same distance from the door as he was. Billy saw that he wouldn't make it, that she would get there before him, and sent a silent plea to Whoever might be listening, that Rebecca make it out alive—

—and then he saw her, not behind the south door at all, but half across the room, her shotgun trained on the leech queen, her back to the central incinerator. Billy realized that she must have run out again while the monster had been busy throwing him against the wall.

He screamed for her to get back to the door, but she ignored him, firing at the queen as she charged toward Billy. With each shot, handfuls of leeches flew from the massive body, but for every one lost, a half dozen more were clambering on. On the fourth shot, the queen turned toward her, hesitating, as if unable to decide who to go after.

"Get in!" she shouted. "I'm on my way!"

Billy ran for the door, hoping to God she had a plan. She continued to fire at the creature, pump and shoot, pump, shoot—and then there was nothing but a dry *click* that Billy could hear across the room, the sound of inevitable defeat.

The leech queen heard it, too, and started for her, her body continuing to grow, to pick up mass as she lurched wetly forward. Billy had reached the south door and stood there, adrenaline pouring through his body, fumbling through his pack for the last two Magnum rounds.

"Run!" he shouted, but Rebecca ignored him, not moving at all. She wasn't reloading, wasn't even reaching for the handgun as the queen approached. Instead, she hefted the shotgun by its barrel, stepped back so that she was touching the incinerator wall— and drove the heavy stock through the sheet metal of a heat duct, popping one of the panels out with an aluminum *crunch*. Burning matter spilled out across the floor. Rebecca jumped into the midst of it, kicking wildly, driving lumps of flaming synthetics and rubbish into the nearest wave of leech bodies.

The queen shrieked, ceased its advance, still well away from the sudden fire. Scorched leeches scurried to their father-queen, tried to climb the towering body, to find solace there, but brought pain with them as they flocked together, attaching to the mobile hive. The queen's shriek grew in intensity as smoking, burning leeches joined her, damaging her, making her writhe in what Billy hoped was insufferable agony.

Rebecca saw her chance and took it, running for the south wall as the queen tore at herself, screaming. Billy emptied the revolver on the floor, dropped the last two rounds into the chamber and snapped it closed, holding it on the queen as Rebecca ran past her—but the queen was beyond caring, at least for the moment, parts of her insane body turning black, melting, running like molasses to pool on the smoldering floor.

Billy kept the Magnum trained on the contorting queen until Rebecca was past him and through the door. He quickly backed in after her, and she slammed the door closed.

He took a deep breath, felt the pain in his ribs, in his arms and legs, his head, a dull agony in every pore of his body—until he turned around, and saw what Rebecca was pointing at, a smile of surprised delight on her shocked, smudged face. His pain dropped away, became nothing but a nagging background to his own sudden relief.

They'd shut themselves into a platform elevator shaft. One that went up—and from the depth of the wide tunnel that stretched away from them at a diagonal, leading toward a circle of light far, far above, the platform appeared to go all the way to the surface.

They grinned at each other like children, too dumb with happiness to speak, but only for a few seconds. Their smiles broke as the dying queen roared, her horrible voice carrying from the next room, reminding them how close they still were to dying themselves.

Without saying a word, they ran to the platform, ran to the standing console that controlled the elevator. Billy studied the switches for a beat, then, with a silent prayer for deliverance, snapped the power on.

The platform started to climb, carrying them up and away from the nightmare. Or so they believed.

Sixteen

The agony was magnificent in its measure, killing her with an intensity beyond any she'd ever known. The burning children clung to her, starved for release, and as they touched her, touched their siblings, they passed their pain on in a wave that would not cease. It went on and on until parts of the collective gathered and fell away, dying, melting, her children sacrificing themselves so that she might live. Slowly, slowly, the agony receded, trained away from the physical, became the suffering of loss, of infinite sorrow.

As the injured pulled away, left her enveloping arms to die alone, the rest of the children came forward, singing, crooning to her, easing her torment as best they could. They engulfed her, soothed her with their liquid kisses—and by their sheer numbers, they overtook her. It only took a moment. The queen lost her identity as Marcus had lost his, giving over to the hive, becoming more. Becoming all.

The allness of the new creature was whole and healthy, a giant, different than before. Stronger. It heard mechanical sounds nearby. It reached inside itself, accessed the mind for information, understood—the murderers were trying to flee.

They would not escape. The hive gathered itself on a thousand supple limbs and went after them.

Neither of them wanted to think about running into any further trouble, but they had to assume the worst. Rebecca checked the handguns while Billy loaded the shotgun, the two of them calling out the dismal numbers—fifteen nine-millimeter rounds left, all total. Four shotgun shells. Two Magnum rounds.

"We probably won't need them anyway," Rebecca said hopefully, staring up at the growing circle of light. The elevator was slow but steady; they were already halfway to the surface, would be there in just another minute or two.

Billy nodded, holding his left side with one dirty hand. "Think that bitch cracked one of my ribs," he said, but smiled a little, also looking up at the light.

Rebecca stepped toward him, concerned, reaching out to touch his side—but before she could, an alarm started to blare down the shaft. Each door they slipped past now had a red light flashing over it, casting crimson splotches of color over the rising platform.

"What—" Billy started, but was interrupted by the calm, feminine voice of a recorded loop.

"The self-destruct system has been activated. All personnel must evacuate immediately. Repeat. The self-destruct system—"

"Activated by who?" Rebecca asked. Billy shushed her, holding up one hand, listening.

". . . immediately. Sequence will commence in— ten minutes."

The lights kept flashing, the siren blatting, but the voice stopped. Billy and Rebecca exchanged a worried look, but there wasn't much they could do . . . And they'd be long gone in ten minutes, God willing.

"Maybe the queen—" Rebecca said, not finishing the thought. It seemed unlikely, but she couldn't think of how else the system might have been triggered.

"Could be," Billy said, though he looked doubtful. "Anyway, we'll be out of here before it happens."

She nodded—and they heard the crash below, the thundering, squealing rip of metal, of incredible ruin at the base of the elevator shaft.

They both looked down, found spaces in the platform's partial grid flooring, saw what was coming. It was the queen—only not the queen. This was much, much bigger, and a hell of a lot faster, a giant dark mass pulling itself after them.

Rebecca looked up, saw how close they were. *Just one more minute and we'll be out—*

She looked down again, her breath catching as she saw how close it already was. She had the image of a crashing wave, black and alive, opening up as it sped toward them, revealing more blackness inside—

"Oh, shit," Billy said—

—and the platform upended, broke through a wall, pitching both of them off.

Rebecca landed on her side, hard, immediately got to her feet, still holding on to the shotgun. Billy was getting off the floor a few meters away, concrete, painted yellow lines radiating out from beneath his feet—

Helipad. Underground helipad.

They were in a vast room, no helicopter in sight but plenty of random mechanical equipment strewn about, the small islands of metal only emphasizing the room's spaciousness. What little light there was came from a few stray shafts of sunlight coming down from the motile ceiling—which meant they were only a single floor from the surface. It took Rebecca the space of a heartbeat to see where they were, a second beat to locate the queen. What the queen had become.

It was crawling out of the ragged hole in the wall where the elevator platform had come through, flopping masses of tentacles over the broken pieces of metal and stone. It was like some crazy optical illusion, watching as it pulled itself from the shaft, its colossal form just coming and coming. The thing that finally expelled itself onto the concrete floor was as big as a moving van, long and low and seething with twisted vines of leech matter.

Rebecca could only stare—and was nearly jerked off her feet when Billy grabbed her arm, pulling her away.

"There's a staircase over there!" He motioned vaguely at an EXIT sign across the room, what seemed an incredible distance away—

—and as if it could hear them, could understand, the queen monster moved, heaved its great bulk across the floor with surprising speed, heading off their escape route. It half turned back toward them, tentacles whipping about its shapeless head, a thick puddle of blackish goo spilling out from beneath its hideous frame, and started to rear up—

—and then squealed, pitching back and forth, a high, hissing noise erupting from its squalid body. Smoke actually started to rise from its back, from where—

Sunlight. A shaft of sunlight, thin but bright, lay across the beast's back. The creature sidled to one side, moving out of the light, and started for them again.

Billy grabbed her again, pulled her back. The self-destruct alarm continued to bleat, echoing through the helipad—and the female voice calmly informed them that they now had eight minutes before the sequence would commence.

"It can't handle sunlight!" she shouted, as she and Billy both turned, started to run. They headed for the room's northwest corner, the farthest from the monster as it humped toward them, twining between the stray beams of light. It wasn't as fast as it had been in the elevator shaft, less to push against, but it could almost keep up with them running.

"Any idea how we open the roof?" Billy asked, shooting a look behind them, steering them more north.

"Power's out," she panted. "But there should be manual latches, probably hydraulic. If the roof's on an incline, it'll slide open when we unlock them. We can hope."

"Do it," Billy said, visibly winded. "I'll try and keep her distracted."

Rebecca nodded, looking back at the creature. It had fallen behind, but it wasn't flagging, wasn't struggling to catch its breath the way they were.

She headed for a likely looking panel on the nearest wall, as behind her, Billy turned and started to fire the nine-millimeter.

The hive went after them, shedding matter from its back where the light had touched. Its consciousness wasn't entirely animal, nor human, but possessed elements of both. It understood that its home was threatened, that another force would destroy its shelter, soon. It understood that sunlight meant pain, even death. And it understood that the two humans that ran before it were the cause of it all, were the instrument of its imminent destruction.

One of the humans stopped, aimed a weapon, fired. Projectiles pierced its outer flesh, wounding, but did not penetrate to the core. As with the sun burns, the creature shed the injured matter and continued on, gaining quickly now, close enough to smell the human's terror. It lunged forward, knocking him down.

Shit!

Billy hit the ground as the queen monster jumped at him, one of the waving tentacles lashing his feet out from under him. He tried to roll away but it had his right ankle in a firm grip. Cursing, Billy pushed himself closer to the mass of the creature, brought his other heel down on the bunched tentacle as hard as he could, and again. The appendage retracted, the monster thrashing away from him.

Billy sprang to his feet, spotted Rebecca at the west wall, messing with a control panel. He turned east and ran, looking back to make sure the thing was on his trail.

"Sequence will commence in—seven minutes."

Lovely. It never rained but it goddamn poured. Billy ran faster, pushing himself, the monster trailing too close for comfort.

When he'd gotten far enough to risk it, he turned, saw Rebecca at another control panel across the room. The monster lunged for him but was too far away to reach, its outstretched limbs still a meter away. Billy got off a shot into what seemed to be its face, then turned and ran again, stumbling on rubbery legs. The thing came after him, seemingly inexhaustible.

Come on, Rebecca, he pleaded silently, forcing himself to go faster.

Rebecca reached the fourth and final latch as the recorded loop told them that they had six minutes left. She grabbed the small wheel that served as the manual key, twisted—

—and it was stuck. Not entirely, but it took all her strength to manage just a half turn. She strained, felt her muscles scream for leniency as she got another half turn, *almost there—*

"Rebecca, move!"

She shot a look back, saw that somehow, the queen monster had gotten close, too close; it would be on her in thirty seconds—but she couldn't, *wouldn't* run, knew that they couldn't afford the time it would take to circle around, to try again.

Billy was firing, the sound of the bullets hitting liquid flesh terrifyingly immediate. She didn't even look, knew she'd lose her nerve if she saw how close it actually was.

"Come *on!*" she screamed, pulling at the obstinate wheel with all she had—

—and it came unstuck, even as a thick, wet limb wrapped around her left ankle, horribly alive with slick, diseased movement—

—and with a heavy squeak of powdering rust, the heavens split wide, raining light over them all.

The light! The light!

The hive screamed as death rained down, first poaching its skin, then boiling it, thousands of individual leeches dying, falling away, the burning worse than fire because it was everywhere, all at once. It tried to escape, to find shelter from the torture, but there was nothing, there was nowhere.

The two humans ran, disappeared through a hole in the wall, but the creature didn't notice, didn't care. It twisted and turned, giant sheaves of flesh scraping away, layers of its body smearing across concrete, exposing the pulsing pink center of itself to the cruel, killing light, the disinfectant light of day.

By the time the building exploded a few minutes later, there was hardly anything left of it—only a handful of straggling leeches, confused, drowning in the lake of death that had once been their father, had once been James Marcus.

SEVENTEEN

They half ran, half staggered away, weaving between tree trunks in the cool morning air, the experience for Billy crazy, surreal—from shooting at giant leech monsters in the dark to a run in the woods, birds singing their morning songs overhead, a light breeze ruffling their dirty, matted hair. They kept moving, Billy silently counting down, until he got somewhere near zero.

He stopped, looked around as Rebecca also halted, breathing heavily. They'd come out of the woods to a small clearing, high on a hill that overlooked the eastern Arklay forest.

"Here looks good," Billy said. He took a deep, cleansing breath and dropped, sprawling on the ground, his muscles cheering. Rebecca did the same, and a few seconds afterward, the countdown was over.

The explosion was massive, shaking the ground, the roar of it washing across the forest, over the valley beneath them. After a moment, Billy sat up, watched the smoke billowing up over the treetops. As tired as he was, as sore and hungry and emotionally drained, he felt at peace, somehow, watching the smoke of that terrible place drift off into the new day. Rebecca sat with him, also silent, her expression almost dreamy. There was nothing that needed to be said; they'd both been there.

He absently scratched at his wrist, at a tickle there—and the handcuffs fell off, landing in the grass with a muffled *clink*. Billy smiled. At some unknown point, the second cuff must have come loose. Shaking his head, thinking of how nice it would have been to have lost them about twelve hours before, he tossed them toward a stand of trees. Rebecca stood, turned away from the smoke, shading her eyes.

"That must be the place Enrico was talking about," she said. Billy forced himself to stand, moved to her side. There, maybe a mile or two away and well beneath their vantage point, was a huge mansion, shrouded with trees. Its windows glared against the morning light, giving it a closed and empty look.

Billy nodded, suddenly not sure what to say. She'd be wanting to get to her team. And as for him . . .

Rebecca reached over and grasped his dog tags, tugging them firmly. The chain gave, popped free, and she fastened the tags around her own slender throat, looking out at the mansion.

"Guess it's time to say good-bye," she said.

Billy watched her, but she didn't look at him, only stared at her next destination, that silent house half hidden by trees.

"Officially, Lieutenant William Coen is dead," she said.

Billy tried a laugh, but it didn't take. "Yeah, I'm a zombie now," he said, a little surprised at the sudden wistful feeling in his chest, in his gut.

She turned, met his gaze, held it with her own. He saw honesty there, and compassion, and strength—and he saw that she, too, felt the same strange longing, the same vague sorrow that had dropped over him like a soft shadow.

If things had been different . . . If circumstances weren't what they are . . .

She nodded, ever so slightly, as if reading his mind, agreeing with what she read there. Then she straightened, her head high, her shoulders back, and snapped a salute, still looking into his eyes.

Billy mirrored her posture, returning the salute,

holding it until she dropped her hand. Without another word, she turned and walked away, heading for a gently sloping decline among the trees.

He watched her until she disappeared, lost to the shadows of the woods, then turned, looking for a path of his own. He decided that south sounded pretty good, and started walking, enjoying the warm sun on his shoulders, the song of the birds in the trees.

EPILOGUE

The distant explosion reached the Spencer estate, shook it so very slightly. Dust shifted on tables. Dirt trickled in the underground tunnels. And the creatures that still lived there turned blind, dead eyes to the windows, to the walls, listening, groping in the darkness, hoping that the very slight movement meant that food would be coming soon.

They were hungry.

ABOUT THE AUTHOR

S.D. (Stephani Danelle) Perry writes multimedia novelizations in the fantasy/science-fiction/horror realms for love and money, occasionally in that order. She's worked in the universes of *Resident Evil*, *Aliens*, *Xena*, and, most recently, *Star Trek;* she has also written a few short stories and translated a couple of movie scripts into books. Danelle, as she prefers to be called, lives in Portland with an incredibly patient husband, and their two ridiculous dogs. She and her husband have recently been joined by the best baby ever, Cyrus Jay.